TWISTED HEARTS

BOOK THREE IN THE SAVAGE HEARTS SERIES

MARY E. TWOMEY

Copyright © 2020 Mary E. Twomey
Cover Art by Emcat Designs

For information:
http://www.maryetwomey.com

For Carla.

Who loves cars, and Mommy.

TWISTED HEARTS

Sometimes the road ahead twists in unexpected ways.

Adelita's new life was supposed to be easier, now that she left the village. But the normal life she craved doesn't last for long. The Kalku won't stop until they have her in their clutches, making any sort of freedom impossible.

While escape seems like the best option, Adelita knows that the time is coming for her to stand and fight for the family that found her...

...and the family she didn't know she had.

1

HIDDEN

ADELITA

When I stretch my arms over my head, I'm careful not to bump my hands to the ceiling. The bed I've been given is tucked into the corner of the attic in the bungalow, so I have to watch myself to make sure I don't bash my head or hands on the ceiling every morning.

You only learn that lesson the hard way once (I hope).

It has been a week since Fernanda brought me into her home. It's not every stranger who sees a woman on the verge of a nervous breakdown, being chased by three men, and drives her off to her home, no questions asked.

Fernanda lives far away from Cáceres, which is just about the best gift in the world.

Actually, a better one would be for me not to be in this mess in the first place. That would mean I'm not Máximo's daughter—a man who is bent on gleaning power at all costs. That would also mean the Kalku aren't hunting me. The savage miscreants are trying to find me, either to bring me to Máximo, or because they want to tear my heart out of my chest, boil it down and drink the broth so they can gain my superhuman strength.

Whatever their motivation, I am glad I'm off their radar, tucked away in Fernanda's home as I am.

If I wasn't in this mess, though, I wouldn't have met the guys. I miss them terribly, but it is better this way. I'm not used to people this entwined in my life. Santos, Cruz and Rafael lodged themselves in my heart, so I knew I had to get out of there. Moving around all the time growing up made me hardwired for flight, rather than fight.

When it became clear that the Kalku will never stop coming after me, I decided it was time to cut and run. It's the only way to keep the Kalku from taking the guys down in their attempt to capture me.

I just didn't expect it to hurt this much.

It's good that I'm away from them, painful as it is. I don't want to be the one to invite danger into their lives. The Kalku are after me, and they are not going to stop. I am Máximo's daughter. The more I distance myself from them, the safer they will be.

I wonder if Rafael is back at the village, or if he is out in the world, trying to find a real girlfriend who will love him for the amazing goofball he is.

I wonder if Cruz thinks I'm angry with him, or if he even cares. I very much doubt my opinion of him registers in the slightest. He should have told me sooner about my parentage, yes, but I don't hate him for it. There are many reasons to loathe Cruz, but right now, none of them seem all that important.

Everything is secondary to the heartbreak that is finding out my father is the king of all the bad guys, and third to the pain of missing the guys.

I try not to wonder about Santos. I touch my lips and still recall the taste of his kiss as I stare at the unpainted wooden walls of the bungalow.

I shouldn't have run out on him with no explanation. Of all of them, he's the one I should have stayed for.

But I didn't. I ran away.

It's for the best. If I had stayed, that would be selfish. I would be leading the Kalku straight for the guys. I am too infatuated with Santos to let him come to harm.

When faced with the impossibility of my parentage, I had two choices: act or accept. I didn't know what to do, so I ran from the whole thing, hiding out here, where nothing and no one can chase me down.

I can sink quite nicely into my denial out here, where Fernanda knows nothing of the demons that haunt me.

I shake my head at myself and stand from the bed.

Santos will move on, and so will I.

Even if this is the seventh day in a row I tell myself this mantra, one day, it will be true. As it stands right now, I miss Santos horribly.

I flit down the steps, doing my best not to make the wood creak. I don't like waking up Fernanda, but it's hard to tell when she's home and when she's not. Being a nurse, her hours are sometimes graveyard and sometimes during the day. It's cruel, switching a person's schedule so drastically all the time like that.

We drank tea together yesterday and had a good gripe about the system that undervalues her, when she is clearly amazing.

Taking in a stranger without hesitation puts Fernanda on the shortlist for sainthood in my book. She hasn't pressed me to spill more information than I am ready to divulge, and in return, I have been looking for work in her area, so I'm not a burden.

Fernanda insists that she has been looking for a roommate, but I'm certain she was envisioning a roommate who could chip in for rent.

After a shower and a quick breakfast, I head out down the street and make my way into town. Sure, there's a bus that could take me, but I have a thing about busses.

After watching my mama die in the bus crash I narrowly escaped from, I'm okay with being a little superstitious and taking the long road.

Fernanda loaned me some of her clothes she doesn't wear anymore, so I have three whole outfits. I like to think the baby blue t-shirt and the slightly loose jeans are the business suit I would normally wear when applying for jobs. But as I am applying for things outside of my normal field, the pretending might not be necessary.

If the Kalku or Máximo are still hunting for me, they might look for me in mental health facilities, where I could use my hard-won degree.

I can still listen to people and build them up while bagging their groceries. I'm sure I can make that happen. I need to connect with people that I can also keep at a distance. Connect and release, connect and release.

That was the problem, living with the guys: each time there was a connection, they stuck deeper in the unfeeling crevices of my heart. I couldn't release them as easily.

I fill out an application at the first grocery store I come to, giving them a fake name, Fernanda's phone number and address. I make it to four stores before I realize I've wandered perhaps too far from Fernanda's home, so I turn back around.

It's hard to keep my mind from wandering back to the guys. It doesn't matter how much I miss them, or even if I regret leaving. I couldn't find them if I tried. I vaguely know where the Cáceres tribe was located. I never drove there myself, and the details are lost in the fuzziness of an endless series of road trips, where all the streets sort of blend together in your mind.

My chest aches to be near Santos.

No. This is better. I shouldn't be with them. The Kalku are trying to find me. Máximo wants me brought to his island. I'm... it's safer for them to be away from me. I love them enough to distance myself so they don't live a life hunted.

My footsteps quicken. Even though it's barely noon, and the small town streets are not at all sketchy, anxiety has been bred into me over these past several weeks. The phantom feeling of being watched creeps up my spine. Though my head darts around, confirming no one cares that I'm here, I still feel the danger.

By the time I reach Fernanda's home, I'm out of breath and scared of my own shadow. I lock the door behind me, leaning against it as my chest heaves.

This didn't used to be me.

I'm a therapist who likes to knit. I live alone and feed stray cats that wander into the alley.

After a few beats, I gather enough of my bearings to breathe without panic.

I can still be me. I can still do the things I love.

Fernanda left her laptop for me, in case I wanted to apply for things online. I was wary to leave any sort of digital footprint at first, but the more I think about it, the less concerned I am with someone tracking me down online. The Kalku live in caves and Máximo lives on an island. The only thing I've seen the guys use their phones for is actual phone calls and texting.

A niggling thought itches the back of my brain: the Kalku put a tracker in my phone once, so they're more computer adept than your average caveman.

I ignore the hesitation in my gut and assume I can apply for jobs online without anyone tracking me down.

And I know exactly where I want to apply.

Therapy online isn't the same as meeting with someone in person, but it fulfills that need inside of me to listen to a person's journey and help them figure out which foot they want to put down in the sand to start out on a new direction. It makes me come alive to help a person find their path.

My smile comes naturally as I fill out applications to a few different online therapy support sites. I even counsel a few of their dummy patients, so they can see what sort of life advice I give in order to further vet my skills.

The three-day wait time is apparently just a formality, because the very next day, I have a job offer that I happily accept.

"I've never seen someone so happy to get a job before. Good for you, girl!" Fernanda applauds me as she finishes her coffee, her umber skin beautiful when framed by the light coming in from the kitchen window. Her home is bright, just like her personality. The cheery buttercup yellow walls add to my happiness.

I try to keep my tears demure, but they come in spluttery gusts because I am so relieved to be back in my element. "Thanks. Feels like a weight has been lifted off my shoulders."

Fernanda tilts her head to the side, her black hair pulled in a bun to reveal a slight smile. "It's a whole new life, Adelita." She rinses out her coffee mug and sets it in the sink, blowing me a kiss before she leaves. "Working a double today, but fair warning: I'm waking you up when I get home so I can hear all about your first day on the job."

"Deal." After Fernanda leaves, I scrub the tears from my face as best I can. My work day starts in half an hour, and I'd like to get all the chores done first. I start with the dishes, then I shine the sink. Even though I've vacuumed every day I've been here, I figure another time is just good practice. I don't mind dusting again, either, since Fernanda goes wild when things are perfectly cleaned. It's the little things I try to do to pay her back for her kindness.

When it's time to meet my first patient, I couldn't be more excited. I bounce in my seat as I turn on the laptop and sign in to the portal, trying to look professional and not overly giddy at being back at work, however remotely. My long inky hair is swept into a bun, and I smooth out any wrinkles from my black t-shirt. Fernanda let me borrow a scarf of hers, which I think makes the whole getup look stylishly casual instead of just casual. I want my patients to know I'm showing up for them. I care about them. I showered for them.

They matter.

The countdown starts, and I straighten my posture.

When the feed connects, my very first patient comes into view.

Her shoulder-length curls spills down on the left side of her visage, giving me a blast of her high cheekbones and quizzical face.

My stomach hollows out as my eyes widen. I grip the sides of the laptop with sudden angst. "Eva?"

Cruz's sister, the eldest daughter of the chief of the Cáceres tribe, looks at me with worry lining her pretty eyes. "Adelita, thank goodness. I've been searching for you for a week!"

2

―――――――

OUR GIRL

CRUZ

I'm an ass. That's really nothing new, and not a huge revelation for me, but every time I think of Adelita running away, I realize how horrible I've been to her. So what if she cries too much? So what if she likes to keep her secrets to herself? So what if she likes to get all cozy with Santos?

Even now as we drive over the speed limit toward the address Eva texted me, I'm not sure I am the person who should be leading the search party. Adelita is going to run the second she sees me, as well she should. I didn't tell her who her father was for like a week when I found out. I've been curt to her, even cruel after she was yanked from her life and dragged into mine.

She chased away La Sayona by holding my hand in the night, and I don't think I ever said thank you. I should have treated her better for staying with me, for risking her sanity so I could finally sleep without torment.

I am a horrible person. I use the smart features on my car to call the florist nearest the village. I ignore Rafael's all-

8

knowing stare as I order two dozen roses and have them sent to the house. Nice guys do that sort of thing, I'm positive. Maybe I'm going overboard, but I've been a week without her. It didn't take one whole day before I realized the error of my ways.

Then, to cover my tracks so no one thinks I'm too soft, I say to the guys, "Rafi, can you text Eva and let her know that the roses are for Adelita from you? Have her set them in Adelita's bedroom."

Santos thanks me from the backseat.

Rafael sends the text to our sister. I can tell by his wry sideways glance that he is not fooled. "How nice of Santos to send his girlfriend roses."

I keep my eyes on the road, ignoring Rafi's insinuation that I'm confusing Santos' girlfriend for my own. I know better than that. I'm not the boyfriend type. I'm the bossy, do-what-I-say type.

Addy is sweet and fiery all at the same time.

Adelita is supposed to be my apprentice, letting me teach her how best to fight the Kalku. Sure, she has superhuman strength, but what if one of them tries to choke her out from behind? I taught her how to get out of that one, but things like escape moves take practice and time to perfect.

My foot leans heavier on the gas, coaxing the SUV to barrel along on the highway at just under a hundred miles per hour. We need to find her before the Kalku can. If we were able to track Addy down, chances are they can, too.

They will take her straight to Máximo's island, where we will never see her again. I race toward the address as if Máximo himself is hot on our heels.

She heals people with kisses. Of course, the family doesn't know that. They only know the lie we fed them: that we found a serum that healed up the scarring on Santos' face.

Adelita wants to remain off the radar, so we kept her involvement a secret.

But running away is a little *too* off the radar.

Rafi clutches the side of the door. "Maybe make sure we don't get in a car accident on our way to Adelita, eh, Cruz?"

I don't bother responding. Sweat trickles down the nape of my neck. I've been a week without proper sleep, and I've gone just as long without a woman looking at me like I might be worth a damn. I miss that. I need it.

At Rafi's second insistence, I ease up on the gas, if only because I don't want to waste time being pulled over for speeding.

The guys know better than to bother me with unnecessary chatter when I'm this tightly wound. I should slow down as we get closer to the address, but I can't.

I'm pretty sure I leave tire marks on the driveway as I peel into the quaint bungalow.

I mean, honestly, is this where Adelita has been staying? Was the bedroom she has in our huge home not enough for her?

I tear out of the car and race to the door, not even bothering to knock. I think I startle us both when I barge into the home, finding her with wide eyes at the kitchen table, talking into a laptop screen.

We're locked in one whole second of stunned silence before pure vitriol spills out of my mouth.

It should be sugar, but venom is more my style. "Are you insane? Do you make it a point to sit in an unlocked home? Anyone could come bursting in here!"

"Clearly!" she spouts back, standing and taking a step back. "What are you doing here?" Then her eyes dart to the screen. "Eva, how could you tell them? How did you know my address? I didn't even tell you!"

My sister's voice comes back with a show of repentance,

however insincere. "I'm sorry, Adelita. I helped the guys track you down. We're worried the Kalku will find you. You're not safe out in the open like this. You need to come back to the village. We can protect you."

Addy bands her arms around her torso, shaking her head and gulping back emotion as Rafi stalks past me and scoops her in a tender embrace.

That's what I should have done. Why did I yell at her about not locking the door? I mean, I'm right; she shouldn't be in an unlocked home. But watching her head rest against Rafi's shoulder, I realize that perhaps a greeting would have been better than outright criticism in the first minute we've reunited.

"Baby," Rafael coos.

The whole thing is overkill.

She's still bracing herself with her arms around her middle, as if staving off a breakdown. Her eyes squinch shut as her voice catches. "You weren't supposed to come after me! I was starting over!"

Rafi stiffens, but recovers with grace as his fingers find their way into her hair. "Well, that's why we've come, of course. You had a good idea, hiding out here. We thought we'd join you."

She picks her head up to gape at him. "You did not."

"Absolutely did," Rafi lies. "I've been working too hard. Trying to keep the daughter of Máximo safe is no easy task, especially when she insists on running away." He thumbs at the burgeoning tears under Adelita's eyes and tsks her sadness. "We missed you, *viento*. Don't you know you're one of us?"

Santos stands in the doorway, but stops there, staring at her with unnamed emotions plaguing his features.

Adelita shakes her head. "They're going to come for me. They want to take me to Máximo's island, or tear out my heart, or whatever they plan on doing when they find me. I don't want the three of you to get hurt when that happens. I'm only staying here with Fernanda until I can get on my feet again. Then I will find someplace away from people."

As one body, my shoulders, Rafi's and Santos' all slump.

Of course the reason she left us is altruistic and thoughtful. Of course she ran away to keep us safe.

Only it doesn't work like that.

When I finally speak, my words rasp against my throat. "*We* protect *you*, not the other way around. We've been panicked, Addy. You shouldn't have left us like that. I thought it was me, that you were angry I kept the bit about Máximo being your father from you. Then I worried it was because I pushed you too hard."

My sister's voice pipes in from the laptop. "That probably had something to do with it, Cruz. You could be nicer, you know."

I roll my eyes and close the laptop, effectively shutting out our eavesdropper.

"Those are very good reasons to leave," Adelita agrees, meeting my gaze with unconcealed hurt. "You did push me too hard. You always do. And I deserve to know where I came from. But no, I left because I don't want anyone to hurt you guys. I'm guessing this whole thing isn't going to all blow over someday. I get the feeling the Kalku won't stop until they have what they want."

Rafi kisses both her cheeks and leads her to sit down in the chair at the table in the kitchen nook. He nods to Santos and me, and I take one of the empty seats across from her.

But Santos stands in the entryway still, only letting himself in a handful of steps as he locks the door behind him. He leans against the door, watching her but not communicating in any way.

I wonder if the bags under my eyes are anything to his.

He looks positively haggard with violet shading around his eyes. The stern angle of his jaw doesn't concede an ounce of softening for her, which isn't like him.

Rafi holds onto her hand because that is what you're supposed to do when your friend is distraught. I don't ever remember to do those types of things, so Rafi picks up the slack. "You've been staying with this woman Fernanda, have you?"

We already know as much. We've got a printout of Fernanda's entire profile.

Adelita nods, her chin tilted downward. "She's the woman who drove me away when you three were chasing after me. Maybe I shouldn't have run away like that, but I knew you would never let me just walk away. It's what needed to happen, guys. And after we catch up, it's going to happen again, only this time without the running. You can't be here." Her brows furrow. "Or *I* can't be *there*. However it happens, we can't be near each other."

Rafi runs his thumb over her knuckles. "Why do you say that? It's not as if we're leaving you so we can go off and enjoy a lazy existence. If we don't protect you, then we're going to track down the next person the Kalku are targeting and do what we can to save them. There's no way we're not going to be in their crosshairs—whether or not you're with us."

She closes her mouth, digesting his logic. "I didn't think of that."

"You didn't talk to us." There's a low note of scolding in Rafi's accusation, but he doesn't punish her more than that.

Rafi is better at people than I will ever be.

She leans toward him and all but melts into his arms. Rafi lifts her body and slides her atop his lap, kissing her temple because he's spoiled and always gets what he wants.

I wouldn't know the first thing about getting a woman to sit on my lap.

"I'm sorry," Adelita whispers. "It all got to be too much. Finding out about Máximo being my father? I didn't know how to handle it."

"Aren't you the therapist?" Rafi teases her. "You're supposed to talk things like that through with the people who love you."

I go completely still, my eyes darting to Santos. Do we love her?

Santos clearly does. And Rafi just confessed as much, even if it comes in a very different form than Santos' addiction to her.

Rafi probably just meant himself and Santos. I don't love her. I wouldn't even know the first step of how to measure something like that.

Adelita sniffles in his arms. Man, he coddles her. I'm not sure which one of them irritates me most with this ridiculous display.

Santos signs to me that he's going to pack up Adelita's things, and can I ask her where they are in the house.

"Where are your things?"

She blinks at me. "I didn't come with more than the clothes on my back. My shoes and the jeans I wore here are upstairs, but that's it."

Santos zips up the steps, keeping his gaze from Adelita.

Well, that's curious. I would have thought Santos would be all about the reunion.

Rafi is the best one to lay the truth out for Adelita, so I stick to the background and let him do the heavy lifting. "It's not safe for you out here. If you don't want to stay at the house with us, then we'll set you up in the tribe somewhere. We assumed a lot, taking you into our home. Didn't give you a whole lot of choice in the matter."

My heart feels like that of a ninety-year-old man. The organ tightens and threatens to freeze up at the prospect that she might sleep anywhere else. Doesn't she know that I need her to chase away La Sayona?

Adelita is a limp ribbon in Rafael's arms. "The Kalku will come for me. They'll attack the village if word gets out that I live there. I don't want Roberto, Mira and Cordelia to be in danger because of me."

Rafi's mouth pulls to the side. "I think there's only one way to put your mind at ease. You should come back to the village, but not as a rescue. I think it would be best if you trained with the soldiers. Then you can see firsthand how safe with us you actually are. And if you're worried about the danger you might bring into the village, then the training will help you defend us." He kisses her cheek. "I know that's where you want to be. You want to keep us safe. That's why you left." Then he buries his nose into the side of her face, inhaling the scent of her skin.

Roses. She smells like roses, no matter how long it's been since she's seen a shower.

"You love us," Rafi declares with certainty, pressing her soft spots so she truly considers coming home with us.

I decide to give being helpful a try. "You have a half-sister who's living in the Mendez tribe right now. They rescued her from Máximo's island. I know you didn't have more than just your mom growing up, but you have a blood relative alive right now, and she's going through this, too. She could probably use someone like you."

I watch Adelita's throat constrict as she swallows hard. "What's her name?"

Rafi opens his mouth to answer, but I hold up my hand. "I think she should tell you that. If you don't want us keeping secrets from you, that's fine. I'm telling you that a blood relative of yours is scared and all turned around in the Mendez village right now. It's to you if you ever learn her name, and you're not getting it until you ask her."

Adelita straightens in Rafi's arms so she can scowl at me. "Are you serious?"

I shrug. "Seems that way. It's her name. It's not mine to give out at random."

Adelita turns back to Rafi. "Is she okay?"

Rafael grins at her. "I'm not telling you a single thing. Cruz is right. It's her story, and she should tell it to you, not us. If you want to get to know your half-sister, then we should get going back to the village."

Adelita leans her forehead to Rafi's and closes her eyes. "I left because I love you all. I don't know what the right thing to do is anymore."

Rafi smooches her lips. I'll never understand how he gets away with doing that so often. He needs to find himself a real girlfriend—someone to spend all that flirty energy on. It's clear she's already taken.

By Santos.

Rafael brushes his nose across hers. "I vote for coming back to Cáceres so you can train with Tio Bruno and learn how to keep us safe. I vote you learn to protect yourself so you can stay alive and escape the Kalku when they pounce again." Rafi kisses her once more as Santos jogs down the steps. "I vote for whatever gets you to come home with us. Don't make me live with a bunch of unshaven, unshowered slobs. You smell like lilies, and I miss it."

"Roses," I correct him without thinking. My grimace must be obvious, because I feel it from head to toe. I shouldn't know what she smells like, and I definitely shouldn't have commented on it.

Rafi's mouth forms an "O" shape while he laughs through his nose at my slip. "Roses, eh?" Then he buries his face in Adelita's neck, drawing out her giggles. "Mm. Maybe you're right, Cruz. Maybe our girl smells like roses, not lilies."

Our girl.

I like the sound of that far too much.

Immediately, I backpedal, my cheeks hot with embarrassment. "Whatever. Let's go."

Adelita stands and crosses the room. "I should probably change, so I don't run off with Fernanda's jeans."

Santos hands over her shoes and jeans, but moves to the bathroom down the hallway, searching it for enemies, and also exits, before she can enter.

They still haven't spoken to each other.

The three of us are silent as she changes, because we all know she could bolt again. Tio Bruno tore us a new one when he learned we lost our charge. If we come home without her... well, that's just not an option.

Letting Rafi handle finessing this was a good plan.

I pull out a handful of bills and set them on the kitchen table to pay Fernanda for housing our girl.

Our girl.

Darn you, Rafi. I need to stop thinking like that.

When Adelita emerges, she eyes the money on the table. In her black t-shirt and jeans, sans scarf, she looks like she belongs with us. Her long, black hair is swept into a bun, making her appear poised and ready for anything. For her to entertain living long-term in another locale? I can't believe we stayed apart this long.

I watch her scribble out a note to the homeowner, and even go so far as to read it over her shoulder to make sure there's nothing damning in there. "Let's go," I urge, moving toward the door.

No sooner do I open it, than an arrow comes flying past me, landing with a thunk in the wood of Fernanda's wall.

I swear as I slam the door shut. "Everyone down!"

They all hit the floor on my command, even Addy. "What's going on?" Adelita's voice is shaky with fear.

I pull a dagger from my sheath. "Looks like we weren't the only ones tracking you."

My jaw tightens when I realize that we led the Kalku right to her.

3

MAN OR PET
SANTOS

My entire body turns to stealth, mutating into my wolf form. Rafi's got Adelita under his arm on the kitchen floor, so she's secure. Now we just have to figure out how to get out of here.

Cruz peeks out the window, crouching to make sure he's not seen. "It's the Kalku. If I can get to the car, I can bring it closer to the door, so you all have a better chance of escape."

Adelita is firm in her protest. "No! We have to take care of them. We can't just run. Otherwise they might come after Fernanda."

Cruz's eyebrows lift appreciatively in her direction. "Never pegged you to be the one voting for more violence."

"Well, here we are, so what's the plan, Chief?"

The corner of Cruz's mouth twitches. "I haven't got one yet."

I'm not one for waiting around while the future leader of the tribe is locked in a stalemate. It's easy to transform just long enough to open the back door and slip out into the mid-morning light, and even easier to get back onto all fours.

Though the Kalku know what my animal looks like, it's still easier to be stealthy as a wolf.

Four members of the Kalku are on the front lawn, weapons drawn. I don't recognize these men in cut-offs and camo. I could ask them what they want, and probably should. But all I see are weapons poised at my family.

I don't hesitate to go for the throat. The one nearest to me isn't prepared to defend himself against my sharp canines, nor my lithe form that tackles him to the grass. Adelita isn't watching, so I don't worry about being too savage and scaring her off.

Maybe it's cruel to tear out a man's throat. Then again, maybe it's poetic. Though these aren't the ones who cursed me, they are all the same in their beliefs that those lesser than them have no value. I wonder how many slaves they have in their cave.

It's for those hidden cave slaves that I move to the next man, who's fumbling through his terror of seeing his friend's blood and sinew dangling from my maw as I run at him full-force.

A man's face shreds easily, no matter how well he's been trained. Regardless of your upbringing, your face can still be turned to ribbons of flesh. It's the great equalizer.

The other two advance as I tear out the second throat. I'm running on a high now. There's something about taking away a person's ability to speak that tastes like delicious vindication.

Cruz barrels out with murder in his eyes. He's focused, and I can see the clear path he has chosen before he collides with the tallest of the two men.

I go for the other, almost laughing at the knives that come out. They will become mine, and so will this third throat. I will collect all the throats of the Kalku, as if any of them will make me able to speak. After this, I will still be mute, but there is part of me that wishes I could stock up the throats of my enemies, and with every one, I could get closer to my liberation.

Cruz and I finish them off, and then drag their bodies into their car. That will be unpleasant for Fernanda to find, no doubt, but slightly less horrifying than them strewn about her front lawn. I duck behind the open car door and turn back into my man form, so I can be more helpful with cleanup.

"That was awesome. I miss a quick takedown. Good job, man." Cruz slaps my hand and brings me in for a hug, but I don't feel cheered by the motion.

I haven't been cheered by much lately. I thought I would bounce back once I saw Adelita, but everything aches whenever I look at her face.

I didn't take proper care of her. She felt she had to run away to keep us safe. She doesn't understand that, with me, she will always be protected. She doesn't have faith in my abilities as a guard.

Part of me hopes she was watching that swift victory. In fact, emboldened by the fight, I march straight into the house and help her up off the floor, where she is on her hands and knees. The only silver lining to the sight is the realization that her shoulder has healed enough for her to have regained some mobility.

The happy thought evaporates quickly as I take in the spectacular nature of her beauty when set against the backdrop of this average suburban setting. This house is simple, and she doesn't belong here. Can't she see how wrong this place is for her?

My fingers are punctuated with irritation, which Rafi incorporates into the interpretation for me. *"No matter what, I will always keep you safe. Running away to protect us? Never again."* I mime stabbing myself in the heart. *"You hurt me, leaving like that. No explanation, no reason. You just ran."*

She is still trembling from the angst of being found by the Kalku. "I'm sorry, Santos! I wasn't trying to hurt you. I was trying to protect you."

I slam my palm to my chest. *"That's my job, and one you need to train for before you assume it like some weight you have to carry. I am a person; I'm not your pet you get to feel sorry for and leave without explanation."* I should stop, but now that I'm opening up, it's all spilling out. I cannot go through this again. *"The Kalku used to leave Santiago and me in the cave for days, sometimes weeks on end. We didn't know when they would be back, and they never gave an explanation. I don't want that uncertainty. When Cruz goes somewhere, he takes me with him. If he can't, he tells me why, and when he'll be back. Same as Rafi. You leaving like that?"* I bunch the material over my chest. *"You scared me. You hurt me."*

It's our first fight, and I hate every second of it. But I've worked too hard to be a man and not a savage. I won't have her thinking I'm a meek kitten she has to feed and shelter.

Her tears shatter my bravado. There are only two, but it's enough to crack through the walls of my frustration.

I move to wipe them away, but my hands are smeared with blood.

It's then I realize my whole face and neck are still dripping with crimson. She's scared of me, as well she should be, what with me looking like this.

I turn quickly and beeline to the bathroom, scrubbing my face and hands in the sink until the only blood left is the wetness clinging to my black t-shirt. Even that comes off, so if she ever wants to be near me again, the gore won't stain her.

Maybe I will always be a savage. As I study my face in the mirror, I can see why she pitied me instead of respected me. I can barely use silverware without making a fool of myself.

I grip the sides of the sink, my torso shivering with shame. I don't want to be this way—stuck halfway between belonging in society and never escaping the cave. I yelled at Adelita. Sure, I can't technically do that, being mute, but the sentiment was the same. She is the best thing that's happened to me in years, and I'm blowing it.

But I don't want to be her cat. I want to be her man.

But the way I just spoke to her, I'm guessing I won't be either ever again.

Still, I would rather be nothing to her than be pitied.

I dry off my face and give myself one last look to make sure I appear more civilized than savage, and then open the door.

I startle, wondering just how low my guard was that she was able to sneak up on me.

Adelita opens her mouth to speak, but the sight of my bare chest slams her mouth shut and colors her cheeks a lovely shade of pink. She's embarrassed that I'm partially unclothed.

That's one tally for being a savage. *Come on, Santos.*

When she finally opens her mouth, I'm surprised by the words that tumble out. "You're right. I didn't treat you like a person. Protecting you seemed like the most important thing, even more than communication. I'm sorry I scared you. I won't do that again. If I leave, I'll talk things out with you."

It's better than nothing, though part of me wants to get to the bottom of why she assumes she will want to leave us again.

I nod once to her. *"Thank you."*

Then she does something that nearly crumbles my resolve. When her right arm curves around my neck, part of me doesn't care if I'm her man or her cat, so long as I am hers. She smells like roses; Cruz is right. Filling my senses with her scent is a gift that's more effective at taking me down than any attack could ever be.

My arm curls around her hips to keep her pressed to me for as long as she will tolerate the closeness. It's intimate, her cheek resting on my bare skin. I love the feel of her softness against the unyielding planes of my body. She belongs right here. How can she even entertain otherwise? Does she not feel how very right this is?

I'm in love with this woman. My body craves her close, just like this. I've been cold without her, inside and out.

She tilts her head to the side, exposing her jugular, which is a clear sign of trust. Even though I just tore out the throats of the Kalku, she knows I will always protect and value her voice.

"I'll get better at this," she promises at the exact time I think the same thing to her.

We will get better at communicating. Until then, I'm going to hold her just like this.

4

BACK TOGETHER

CRUZ

The plan was to get Adelita to Santos' curse tree as soon as possible. Her incredible strength is the only thing that can dislodge his curse axe and set his voice free. But on our way, we get a phone call from Tio Bruno, demanding we come home "with the girl."

Her name is Adelita, which he very well knows, but I don't have the gall to talk back to my uncle and my superior.

I switch trajectories only when Santos agrees that we can delay our trip to his liberation.

This had better be important.

Adelita leans forward in her seat. "Can I use your phone, Cruz?"

My brow quirks at her in the rearview mirror. "Who are you calling?"

"Your uncle. Just real quick."

Rafi turns in the passenger's seat to study her sincerity. "What for?"

"I want to know what's so important that we're putting Santos on hold. I think an explanation is okay to ask for. He doesn't know what our plans were, so maybe he wouldn't ask that of us if we told him what we're on our way to go do."

I catch her eye in the rearview mirror. "You're going to tell him everything?"

She snorts. "I never tell anyone everything."

I hate how true that statement is.

Santos signs quickly that he wouldn't dream of defying Tio Bruno like that.

When Rafi interprets for her, she harrumphs. "I'm not going to tell him he's an idiot or anything. Is he really so horribly bullheaded that he wouldn't want all the facts? Is it his-way-or-the-highway, or is it the-best-way-or-the-highway?"

My mouth pulls to the side. It's a fair question, though I'm not disrespectful enough to say so. Before I can protest, Adelita leans forward and sneaks the phone from the center console, distracting me with a peck to my cheek.

Heat flares through my whole body at the sweetness. No one kisses my cheek except for my brothers. No one wants to get near enough to try. But this is something new and different, her playfully pecking affection into my skin. My neck shrinks as a bashful smile replaces my perpetual scowl.

Without meaning to, I reach up and touch the spot where she kissed me, savoring the sweetness because it's so very foreign to me. I am not the man women get all cozy around. I'm the one the villagers respectfully back away from. They know La Sayona haunts me, and they want no part of her cruelty. Can't blame them for that.

Even Eva and Consuela don't bother with tiny affections like that. They know I'm prickly and grant me the space I require from all people.

Then here comes Adelita, trampling over the hedges that everyone knows not to touch.

I'm so distracted that I only just realize she's searching

through my call log and connecting with none other than Tio Bruno. She pushes another button, and my uncle's brusque voice stiffens every spine as it booms through the car over speaker. "Yes?"

I open my mouth, but Adelita speaks first. "Tio Bruno? This is Adelita."

She pauses until he puts words to his confusion. "What can I do for you?"

Well, that's unexpected. When other people say something like that, it's a formality. When Tio Bruno says it, it's an offer and a promise.

He knows she is valuable. We didn't tell him about her strength, or the fact that she tore several curse axes from a tree, but he knows she is Máximo's daughter.

Adelita's cadence is light and friendly. "I wanted to tell you what we're up to, to see if we can delay coming back to Cáceres right away. We wanted to visit Santos' curse tree first. I'm still trying to wrap my mind around the culture here. Is that alright?"

Tio Bruno's reply is so tight, my upper lip curls. "You want to delay coming to the village by almost a week so you can see a tree and get a history lesson? That is a waste of time. I will tell you all you need to know about the curse tree, and you can come straight home."

She hesitates, and I can tell she doesn't want to admit her strength to Tio Bruno, nor the true reason we are visiting the curse tree. I let her keep her secret, because it's hers. Trust is best when it unravels, rather than when it's forced. "Tio Bruno, can you tell me why you need us home right now?"

Another hesitation, which is akin to a slow seethe. She is not his soldier, and she doesn't know enough to be afraid of him, so he can't very well go off on her. "There is something I would like you to see to in the barracks. I could use some help."

A small smile curves Adelita's lips while I drive. "I'm proud of you for asking for help. That's hard to do, you know—admitting you can't do something on your own. If you're stumped, I'm happy to help you however you need. Some things are just plain tricky."

She's not patronizing, I don't think. Or at least, she's not outright telling Tio Bruno he's a wimp who can't tie his own shoes without a woman half his age to help.

Rafi covers his mouth to trap his laughter inside.

Santos looks so frightened, I'm concerned he might pee himself.

Tio Bruno stammers through his response, which is so unlike him, my mouth falls open in astonishment. "Well, it's nothing like that. Nothing I can't do without you."

Adelita jumps on his words with pure sunlight streaming through her tone. "Oh, really? That's wonderful! I knew you could figure it out. Cruz is always saying how brilliant you are, and I'm starting to think he's right. Of course you wouldn't need help from an outsider like me. You probably were just trying to make me feel included. Thank you, Tio Bruno. You're the sweetest ever." She gives a hearty fake laugh that stuns me with how real it sounds. "We'll see you in a week after we visit the curse tree. Do you want me to bring you back a souvenir?"

"What? No!" I can picture his grimace as he entertains such a frivolous offer.

"Alright, have a great day!" Adelita ends the call with a wide grin aimed at our collectively stunned faces. "Not for nothing, but like, half my job consists of convincing people to be better than they currently are. Looks like we've got the week free, boys."

Rafi's laughter bursts out of him, giving voice to the astonishment we're all feeling at her gall. "Did you really just do that? I've never seen Tio Bruno get fleeced so quickly. Oh, that was beautiful, *viento*. That can be my Christmas and my birthday present. Oh, when he's tearing me a new one next time, I'll picture him falling in line for you just like that. Well done, Adelita."

Santos signs to her that he could have waited for her to end his curse.

She puts her hand atop his. "You've waited long enough. I shouldn't have run. I wasn't thinking long-term. The plan was always to free you. I lost sight of that. Please forgive me, Santos."

If he doesn't kiss her, it's a missed opportunity.

Of course he doesn't. He merely holds her hand, twining his fingers through hers in that cutesy way they do when they're together. It's so doe-eyed and juvenile, yet my chest tightens at the sight. It keeps my eyes tethered to the spot where they are joined.

I cringe at the thought of the roses being delivered later today, and no doubt being all wilted by the time we actually get back. I feel stupid now, like I can't even get a cheesy non-gesture right.

We're all very careful with each other now, knowing that at any moment, she could bolt, and would probably have every right to. I've been an ass to her, but I don't exactly know how to correct that, other than not do it going forward.

Then an idea hits me. Even though we've still got half a tank, I pull into the next gas station I come across to refuel. When I hand Adelita a fist of bills, her eyes widen. "Feel like some hot chocolate?"

It takes a beat for her to examine the money and me. No doubt she has to process what I'm saying and parse it for rigid angles that might cut her if she gets too close.

I should probably stop doing that to people.

"Really? Do you want some, too?"

My shoulders are tense at the very mundane exchange. Am I doing it right? Is this what a nice person would do? Is this how a considerate person would sit? "That'd be great. I'm sure Rafi and Santos wouldn't mind something sweet after the dust up with the Kalku."

"On it!"

She likes being helpful, having purpose, adding value to the team. I can see it in the way she lights up.

Before she exits the car, I pause her. "While you're in there, I want you to count how many exits. I want you to count how many people. And I want you to make a list of things that could be used to make impromptu weapons."

I want to grimace away from my words, as she's doing now, but I can't. She's too important not to know the basics of how to stay out of harm's way.

Adelita sits back in her seat. "Let's stop at a different gas station if we've got a tail." Her eyes dart around anxiously.

I hold up my hand to calm her. "There's no tail. I wouldn't send you in at all if there was. Hey," I make my voice sharp so she looks up at me, instead of worrying about her surroundings. When her scared gaze connects with mine, "I'm always watching," tumbles out of my mouth.

It's meant to be a reassurance, but Rafi groans at my ineptitude that makes me sound like a stalker at best, or like someone who's watching for her to slip up at worst.

I quickly backpedal. "I told you I would train you. This is part of that. Wherever you go, those are things to make note of when you visit someplace new." I tick off the basics on my fingers. "Count your exits, count how many people are in your space, and list your potential weapons."

She nods solemnly, now looking at the bills in her hands with a gravity I didn't mean to put there. "Okay. Thanks."

I'm terrible at this. I managed to find a way to ruin hot chocolate.

Santos goes in with her while I refuel, and Rafi gets out to stretch his legs. He doesn't say anything to me, but I feel his silent lecture.

By the time she gets back in the car with the drinks, her happy flourish with adding the caramels and spicy candies is gone. "One exit, four people in the building, and I could use a thing of oil to make the floor slippery, which would give us time to escape."

I nod appreciatively. "That's a good one. I never thought of that. I'm usually looking for sharp things to pierce my enemy with, but stalling them is a good idea. I'll have to remember that."

Her head jerks up. "Really? I did it right?"

"Better than right," Rafi offers, taking his drink from her. "You just taught an old dog a new trick. That's hard to do."

I set my drink in the cupholder and drive us across state lines. I keep us going through the day, and well into the night.

When Adelita's head lolls against Santos' shoulder, I know she won't leave us again.

At least, I hope she won't leave us again.

5

STRENGTH IN VULNERABILITY

CRUZ

The lines on the road start to blur, so I know I've passed the point where I should have stopped for the night.

Ever since Adelita started sleeping near me, I've lost my taste for bare-bones motels. I want a firm mattress with too many pillows. I don't want to worry about cockroaches or idiot teenagers renting a room next to mine to throw a wild party. I want amenities. I want quiet.

I *need* dreamless sleep.

Instead of beating around the bush after we get our keycards and Rafi takes first crack at the shower, I go for a direct request. She knows I need her help. There's no use clinging to pride at this point.

"Adelita, is it okay if we push the beds together? La Sayona noticed you were gone. I could really use a full night of sleep."

Santos tilts his head in my direction, like me being humble and asking instead of demanding is akin to me suddenly sprouting a third arm.

Adelita softens. Whenever she feels anything, her whole

body reacts. Her shoulders lower, her eyes turn doe-ish, and she takes half a step toward me. "Oh my gosh, of course, Cruz. I'm so sorry I left. It seemed like a good idea at the time, but I didn't think through all the angles. I feel horrible. I meant to leave to protect you, but all I managed to do was leave you unprotected."

I hold up my hand to put a cork in her bleeding conscience. "It's not your responsibility to fix what my ancestors broke. But if you don't mind me in your space, I would really appreciate the help."

"Absolutely." Her mouth pulls to the side, and I can tell she's psychoanalyzing me.

Santos signs that he's going to make a lap around the building before we turn in, and then squeezes Adelita's hand before he exits.

I don't expect conversation from her, so when it finds me, I stop all movement.

"Does she hurt you in your dream? How specifically? What can you tell me about La Sayona?"

I blow out a long breath. I really don't want to talk about this. "She didn't leave physical damage this past week. She only does that when she's really worked up. She seemed more out of it the first night after you were gone. Not quite drunk, but definitely labored movements and unfocused blows. Every night, she's grown more clearheaded. Last night, it was business as usual."

"Meaning?"

Adelita wants specifics, and I don't want to give them. But I know that if she wants to know more about me, I can't hold back anymore. I can't demand she tell us about herself and then clam up when the tables are turned. That's not leadership.

She's not asking because she's curious (or at least, not just because of that); she's asking because she's nervous. She wants to know all the people in the room, including the one who haunts me at night.

"Last night, La Sayona came into my head and took a bat to my knees once she got me cornered. She's not a person; she's an apparition, so she can move far faster than a human. She can vanish and then reappear without warning. One time, she reached right through a wall and grabbed me by the throat." I shake my head at myself. "I swear, I'm a decent fighter when it's man-on-man. When it's supernatural ghost on man? It's uneven playing ground."

Adelita plops down atop the mattress, studying my movements while I pull out my pajamas.

That's right; I travel with pajamas now.

"Why is La Sayona afraid of me? I mean, I'm not complaining. Anything that helps you sleep is great. But why me? Isn't she supposed to be angry when a woman sleeps near you? Isn't she supposed to be attacking me?"

I shrug. "I have no idea why it's helping. That's why I reacted so angrily when I woke up and you were in my bed that first couple of times. The first time, she had already attacked me, so I figured she was done for the night, and you'd narrowly escaped her. The second time? She just vanished mid-attack. She got this scared look about her, like a mean parent was calling her name and she was in big trouble or something. It was so weird. When I put two and two together after I woke up and found you and Santos in my bed, I was so scared for you. I didn't want her attacking your brain."

Adelita doesn't respond right away, but reaches out and grips my hand, pulling me down to sit beside her on the bed. We sit there like that, my hand limp and malleable in her lap while she gently plays with my fingers.

Rafi's wrong. She smells like roses, not lilies.

"You don't have to ask anymore," Addy finally says. "I

know it's hard to have to ask for help every night. Just assume that if I'm here and we haven't had a big fight, then I'll sleep next to you."

Tension drains out of me as she begins massaging my palm. There's not a sensual thing about it, but it's downright intimate to me. I don't let people play with my fingers. I don't hold hands.

Not that there's a huge line of women vying for the position.

"I'm not good at this," I admit, as if that should cover all my bases. When it clearly doesn't, I explain. "Being around people. I'm terrible at it. Rafi and Santos are my brothers. Anyone else... I'm no good at people."

"I wonder why that is."

What a therapist thing to say. She doesn't counter my assumption, but turns it back on me.

This sucks.

I take her question and really mull it over, because she's playing with my fingers and I don't want her to stop. "People don't know the kind of stress I'm under. They know the highlights, but not how it affects me day-to-day."

"They don't know, or you don't want them to know?"

Doggone this woman. "Maybe a little bit of both."

"But Rafi and Santos know?"

"They sleep in the same room with me on the road more often than not. My sleeplessness is theirs. But they don't pity me the next day. They treat me like I'm capable, so I remember that I am."

"They don't make concessions for you?"

Again, she stumps me. "Maybe they do. Little ones like looking the other way when I'm short-tempered."

"How often do you think you're short-tempered?"

My voice lowers, not wanting to touch that question with

a ten-foot pole. "Maybe too often. Often enough that they're surprised when I'm not an ass."

"It sounds like you appreciate them."

My voice is rough. I'm not sure how we took a turn down this path. "I do. Whatever the word is for someone who is closer than family, that's what they are to me."

The moment the words come out of my mouth, I realize how true they are. Santos and Rafi are so tightly knit to me that sometimes I don't know where I end and they begin. They've picked up slack for years without complaining or acting like I'm an inconvenience.

Adelita gently coaches me through the moment where I'm utterly stumped by my realization. "Sounds like you love them. I wonder if they know that."

My mouth pulls to the side. "I mean, how could they not?"

She shrugs. "Funny thing about loving someone you're also an ass to. They're left guessing. I wonder if they feel valued."

I swallow hard when she squeezes my hand. Everything in me feels heavy now. If this is what it's like to live with a shrink, I'm not sure how I'll stand much more of it.

Then again, being without Adelita isn't an option. La Sayona aside, I like having her around. I don't know if I like this knot in my chest, but maybe it's the medicine I need.

"You talk to me like you're not afraid of me. Same way you spoke to Tío Bruno."

She blinks up at me, a few whisps of black hair falling to the side. Her lips purse but her eyes appear innocent. "Do you want me to be afraid of you?"

She's so close; I'm certain she can hear my heart hammering against my ribcage. I mean to respond aloud, but my "no" is swallowed because I'm pretty sure she can feel my palms are sweating.

What is wrong with me?

Rafi emerges from the shower in pajamas. His knowing grin breaks my hand out of hers with a jerk. "Shower's all yours. Whichever of you."

"I'll go." I should probably be a gentleman and offer to let her go next, but I have to get out of here. I stand abruptly and nearly run into the bathroom like a scared little boy.

Cold water is the only thing that helps shed the moment from my mind. Half an hour later when we're all showered and ready to turn in for the night, I've managed to fend off any teasing Rafi's tried to shove into his sentences whenever he talks to me.

Santos is less meek now. He's not overly assertive, exactly, but he doesn't want to sleep on her feet anymore and call it good enough. The two queen beds are pushed together, and Rafi is shunted to the outside, instead of enjoying his spot with Adelita's round butt cradled against his lap all night.

Santos curves his body around hers, spooning her and making her look fragile, though we all know she's anything but breakable. Still, he cocoons her, kissing her shoulder because he's allowed to do things like that. Though the connection between them is still on the mend, it's clear they very much belong to each other.

And I get to watch.

Awesome.

I feel stupid, and like I'm a broken third wheel, but Adelita seems to understand this before it can make me surly. She reaches out and brushes her hand over my chest, causing my breaths to stutter.

I don't mean to speak. I'm not even sure I want to. But the moment she brushes her hand over my sternum, stupidity pours out of me and spews itself all over the beige walls. "I appreciate you guys."

Damn this woman.

I barrel through. "Santos, Rafi. You deserve better than

me being a pill to live with. I don't know where I'd be without you. Everyone in the tribe thinks I'm a big deal, but it's only because you two are with me every day. I should treat you better, starting with telling you that you're my family, and I couldn't do any of this unless you were with me. I love you."

I groan aloud at how asinine I sound. I've got to get out of here. I flip the comforter off my body and get out of the bed.

Rafi sits up, his mouth hanging open. Even Santos is gaping at me like I've grown a goiter the size of a fist.

"Are you dying?" Rafi asks, no trace of teasing anywhere in his tone.

"What? No." I snort as I shove on my shoes. "I'm going to get some air."

Rafi holds his hand up. "Wait. What was that about? Why are you being nice?"

As if I needed to feel bad on top of feeling stupid. "I'm not allowed to be nice?"

Santos signs a careful, *"Cruz, did you hit your head? Let me take a look at your pupils. You're not acting like yourself."*

I lean forward on the side of the bed and pinch the bridge of my nose. "Forget I said anything. I take it all back. Can we pretend this never happened?"

At this, Adelita sits up. "No. Don't take a step forward and then run away from the progress. It's one step, Cruz. Just stay here and test out how it feels. Vulnerability isn't weakness. It's the first sign of true strength."

"It feels ridiculous!" I shouldn't raise my voice, but I do. "They know they're important to me. They know I won't go on missions without them. They know they matter. We don't need to talk about it all the time."

Rafi raises his hand. "I didn't know that. I mean, I guessed as much, but it's nice to hear."

Santos signs, *"I owe you my life. Of course I'll go on every mission with you.*" Then his face grows solemn. "*I never dreamed I'd ever be more than a slave, a dog. To hear you say you love me?*" Then he taps his chest to let me know he's too moved for words.

My shoulders slump. "Of course I love you, Santos. I don't even like anyone besides you two." Then I nod at Adelita. "And I guess you."

Adelita rolls her eyes at me. "Thanks."

The corner of my mouth tugs upward, and the two of us share a smirk.

Rafi lays back down, addressing the ceiling. "I don't remember having siblings other than you two. I like to think I traded up."

I crack my knuckles as my mouth draws to the side. "I'll do better at this—better at being your brother. Better at not making your lives miserable. The Kalku should do that without my help."

Rafi lets loose an airy laugh through his nose. "I like that. We don't mind you, Cruz. We get why you're unhappy all the time. But yeah, it's okay to have a good day every now and then. More than being nice to us, that's what we want you to remember."

I take a moment to digest this new information. They are good guys. They don't even care that I've been insufferable; they care that I'm miserable most days.

Rafi clears his throat after I take off my shoes and lay back down. "While we're confessing things, can I say I'm scared of my dragon? I've never known any shifters other than you, Santos, and the way you shift is different than me. It's like walking around inside a wet mattress. Nothing feels natural. I'm afraid I'll press the wrong button, and light the hotel on fire by accident."

Adelita coos her sympathy, but this is something that requires a plan, not just sweetness. I can help with that. "It sounds like you need practice. We haven't exactly given you space to test things out. After Santos gets his curse lifted, I can take you to an open field so we can really see what we're working with."

Rafi exhales like he's been afraid for weeks.

Has he? Did I really not notice?

"That would be great. Thanks, man."

Santos signs that he's more than happy to help, and that he wishes Rafi would have spoken up sooner.

Then Santos signs to us, banking on the assumption that Adelita hasn't picked up enough sign to eavesdrop. "I could use some help with doing this right. I don't know how to be a boyfriend. I don't understand why she's with me. Is it pity?"

Rafi and I both shake our heads like they're tethered to the same string. "Not a chance," Rafi explains. *"She's with you for loads of reasons, one of which is that you treat her with respect and kindness. Stick with that, and you're golden. Anything more complicated is when people go off the rails."*

Adelita frowns. "For the record, I know you're talking about me. It's rude to not interpret if I'm sitting right here. I only caught like, half of that."

Santos responds by dipping his head down and apologizing. Then he sweeps a lock of hair from her cheek and kisses her lips just once, soft and sweet.

Her whole body reacts, her back bowing slightly as her good arm falls back in a show of surrender. A helpless whimper escapes her as she melts into the mattress. I shouldn't watch Santos thumb her cheek, but I can't look away.

She trusts him completely.

When their kiss ends, I sign as much to Santos.

"You're doing it again," Adelita grumbles at me the moment she comes out of her haze of happiness. "It's bedtime, so stop talking about me."

I settle into the sheets as best I can, but part of me feels hollowed out at all this off-beat communication. I suppose I feel lighter, but perhaps too light, like I can't tether myself to the same place I've always been. Now I don't know where I belong, or if I do, I feel strange taking up space in this new arena I haven't thoroughly vetted.

Adelita seems to understand, even though it barely makes sense to my muddled brain. She rolls onto her side, cocooned by Santos, and then reaches out to me, clearing the divide between us.

I expect her to hold my hand, the way she always does to frighten away La Sayona. Instead she tugs me closer, near enough for me to feel her slight tease of breath across my lips. Adelita's hand runs up the length of my arm, soothing me like the wild animal I sometimes am.

"I'm proud of you," she whispers, and then tilts her chin up to kiss me on my nose.

That's all it takes for my entire being to crumple in on itself.

The floating void of uncertainty doesn't matter anymore. The second I slide under the protection of Adelita's arm, my stuttering heart calms in the span of one long, contented sigh.

"There," she says quietly, and I can hear the smile in her voice. "That's better."

Santos merely grants me a tired smile over her shoulder as if to say he totally understands what it is to be calmed by her presence. I'm not sure I should be this close, but neither of them pushes me away, so I greedily gulp up all the contact she'll give me.

Usually I wake with my nose in the crook of her neck, but tonight, her nose finds its way to mine. The softness of her cheek molds itself to my clavicle, her damp hair soaking the shoulder of my shirt.

This is intimate. This is bliss.

Santos reaches over her form to give my bicep a light squeeze of acceptance.

I do the same to him. The two of us hem her in, not as if she's fragile, but because she's treasured. In the span of a conversation, she cracked my sternum wide open and showed me my own beating heart.

I ignore Rafi's wide-eyed shock and close my eyes, soaking in the feel of this woman trusting me enough to be this near. Her knee slides between mine, like it knows exactly where it belongs.

The Kalku will have to go through me to get anywhere near her. I kiss the top of her head as if that's the kind of thing I do at random. Then I drift off into my dreamless sleep.

6

WHO IS RAFAEL
RAFAEL

Everything has been different since that first night. Adelita, Santos and Cruz are so calm; it's almost impossible not to stare. The three of them move in sync now, as if traveling on the same fluffy cloud.

Santos and Adelita are in love, so that's not too shocking. They may not have labeled it that yet, but it's what it is. They're so mindful of each other, holding hands and making considerations for the other.

All of that is sweet, but it's not the reason I stare. The most unnerving change of all is Cruz. It's not how kitten-like he is with her at night, though that's its own freak show, to be sure. What gets me gawking is his total personality transformation during the day.

He asked me to drive, for starters. Usually the control freak would rather drive off the road in a sleepy haze than share the wheel. He's in the passenger seat, half-turned, and signing everything he says, occasionally pausing to show her the sign for a new word twice. He's helping Adelita and Santos learn to communicate without our assistance, which is so selfless, I'm not sure what to do with it. If he was trying to steal her away from Santos, he wouldn't bother building up their relationship. But it's like anything that makes her smile or boosts her confidence is something he jumps to invest in.

It's a good thing, naturally, but it's unlike him.

"You know," I interject, "we're on our way to Santos' curse tree. After the axe comes out of the curse tree, she won't actually need to speak sign."

Cruz frowns, as if I've said something offensive. "Sign is dead useful. It's a secret language only the three of us speak fluently in the entire tribe. The Kalku don't care to learn it, either. It's a tool, Rafi. One more thing in our arsenal that puts us ahead of the enemy."

I consider his logic as I check my speed and slow down a little. "I guess you're right. There have been times that we've signed to each other mid-fight, and it's given us the advantage. Carry on."

I've never seen Santos this relaxed. But each time I glance in the rearview mirror, his head is leaned back against the window. His body is turned sideways on the seat, along with Adelita's, so he can hold her for hours upon hours. Occasionally he strokes his fingers over her arms or plays with her hair, marveling at each portion of her body with which he has been entrusted.

Beneath my confusion, I couldn't be happier to see my best friends—my brothers—finally breathing. Makes me wonder how much of their lives they've spent suffocating.

Cruz speaks up in my direction. "Hey Rafi, turn off at the next exit, okay?"

I do as he requests, grateful at the prospect of being able to stretch my legs soon.

"See that abandoned warehouse? Pull in behind it."

My brow quirks. "Any particular reason?"

"It's a secluded place where your dragon can test his limits a little. The brick wall will hide anything. A building that dilapidated is sure to keep any prying eyes away."

"True that. I can barely look at the structure without cringing. It doesn't look stable. Makes you wonder if it ever was." I'm babbling because I'm nervous. I don't know how use my dragon properly. "You sure about this?"

Cruz nods once, which I know means his mind is already made up.

It's a good idea. I know I shouldn't resist it, but my stomach tightens all the same. I have no idea what I'm doing as a full-blown shifter.

I guess that's why it's a good idea to practice in a controlled setting.

When Santos gets out of the car, he starts in with a litany of questions, his lax demeanor cracking off of him as he transitions into an instructor.

"Do you recognize us when you're a dragon?"

"Yeah, I know who you are, but everything has a red haze around it. So I can see you, and I know I don't want to hurt you, but it takes an extra second for me to make out your faces." I rub the nape of my neck, which is already sweating. "That's going to be a problem."

Santos skips over the roadblock entirely. *"When you're in your animal, I want you to try talking. Mine comes out as a bark, obviously, but I don't know what yours will sound like. We need to get to know your noises. Just like Cruz said about sign language— the more ways we can communicate without the Kalku catching on, the further ahead of them we'll be."*

"Makes sense. I'll give it a try." Practicing talking is a lot less intimidating than breathing fire.

"Can you spot details? If I sign to you, does your brain process the information in the same way?"

"I mean, I don't really know. I haven't spent all that much time as a dragon."

Santos explains. *"For instance, when I'm my wolf, sometimes I think only in verbs, especially when I'm rattled. 'Kill, attack, bite,'— things like that. I can think in full sentences if I make an effort, but it's not my wolf's natural inclination. That took time to build up. You might have to force language on your animal to get him under your control. That's the most important thing in all this. You control your dragon, not the other way around. Otherwise, you're a monster waiting to unleash."*

I nod, taking his advice in and mulling it over. "I didn't realize there was so much to shifting. But you're right. A dragon is an animal that needs a tether." My mouth pulls to the side as I contemplate his words. "My dragon isn't in control, but it's clear I have no idea what I'm doing, so neither of us trust me to drive this thing."

Santos claps his hand to my shoulder and squeezes, signing an abbreviated version of his sentences with his free hand. *"Nature trusted you to give you this animal. Nature knows you are capable of controlling it and using your animal for good. It just takes practice."*

And just like that, a hefty ten percent of my nerves fade away. I'm not an experiment of the Kalku gone wrong. I'm a purposeful part of the world that belongs. "You're right. I can do this. I'll learn."

"And I'll be right here while you do. I had the Kalku to teach me about my animal, and I turned out okay. You have me. You're going to be far better than okay. I will not let you come to ruin, Brother."

Stupid Cruz with his emotional breakthrough. Now I'm getting all choked up. I crash into Santos with a rough hug, grateful for all that he is to me. "Thank you."

Santos' chest vibrates with a silent chuckle as he grips me

like I matter to him. He kisses my cheek, and I love him for it.

The second Santos releases me, Nice Guy Cruz is gone, and Business Cruz is in full swing. "Addy, over here. Near the end of the building, got it?" Before she can protest at him putting her in a position of being protected, he holds up his hand. "We all know you're strong, but that doesn't mean you know how to take a punch. It also doesn't mean any of us have the stomach to watch you get hurt if this goes south. Your shoulder is still on the mend. Safety first."

Her mouth opens, and I can tell she wants to argue, but then she snaps it shut because his reasons are both logical and sweet. She trots to a spot near the end of the boarded-up building, so she can duck out of sight around the corner if needed.

I hate that I am the danger.

Cruz locks his gaze on me and nods once. "When you're ready, shift and don't do anything else. Don't walk. Don't turn around. And don't you even think about breathing fire. We're taking this whole thing as slow as it can possibly go."

I run my sweaty palms over my thighs. I do what I can to push out all the doubts in my head that insist I'll never be worth anything. The worry that I'm ruined after the Kalku got their hands on me isn't going to help in this situation.

Scattered memories spatter themselves all over my brain.

Experiments that involved them slicing a hot line down my shoulder blade.

Being thrown into a pit while the elders did chants over me.

Crying for my mother to find me.

Then crying different tears when I was rescued and she couldn't look at my face.

I wasn't her special buddy anymore. I was special, sure, but for all the wrong reasons.

Don José scooped me in his arms while I screamed for my parents as they drove away. He kept me by his side for months after that, helping me find purpose and value.

And here I am, that trembling five-year-old all over again, hoping the people who have become my world don't reject me when they see the monster I might always be.

"Deep breaths, Rafael," Adelita calls to me. "Close your eyes." When I am too anxious to heed her simple request, she takes a step forward. "Tell me who you are. What makes you, you?"

My mouth pulls to the side. I can practically hear Cruz's internal groan that we're about to talk instead of getting to the action.

Out of curiosity, I entertain her question. "I think I'm fun. Funny. Not sure if there's a difference, but I think I'm both."

Her grin cheers me as she moves toward where I stand with my feet shoulder-width apart. "I agree with that. What else? Who is Rafael?"

"I'm a decent fighter. Wicked with my knives."

She nods. "What else?"

She's close enough now that when I reach out and sweep her up in a short quickstep, she falls easily into my arms. "I'm a terrific dancer."

Her footwork is rigid. Must remedy at a later date.

She laughs, and all three of us loosen up at the sound. "You are. What else?"

My dancing stops, but I keep her in my arms. My next confession is quiet, and comes out like my grief might actually succeed in choking me. "I'm not worth my parents' time."

She tilts her head to the side while Cruz goes off on the rant I know is coming. "Your parents are short-sighted, superstitious idiots that have been banned from the village. You are worth their time, but they are not worthy of yours."

Santos signs as much, but Adelita remains in my arms, not countering my assessment. "That sounds like it hurts."

My throat constricts as I nod. "Hurts all the time."

She breathes deeply, her chest moving against mine, which reminds me to invite ample oxygen into my lungs, granting my mind some space. "Can we try something?"

I have no reason to deny her anything. She asks so sweetly, and I'm nine kinds of vulnerable right now. "Sure."

Her fingers brush through the hair near my temples. "I'm going to take a deep breath. Several. And with each one, I want you to put some distance between yourself and that pain. We're not going to pretend it's not there. We're not even going to try to reason with it right now. We're just going to set it down and take five steps back. We can pick it up again whenever we like, but for today, we're not going to carry it around. Does that sound okay?"

I listen to her because frankly, listening to my own insecurities hasn't done me any favors. My mouth is dry and my palms are sweaty when I finally nod.

On the first long inhale and exhale, she coaches me. "Good, now set that grief down and take one step back. You can still see it. You know it's there, but you're not wearing it. It's not part of your makeup in this moment. It can be later, when you want to pick it back up, but for now, when you look at yourself, it's not there."

I can't believe she's right about this. It's so strangely simple, but mentally putting the rejection down and inching back from it coaxes fresh air into my body.

"I actually do feel lighter. Weird."

"Because you're carrying fewer layers. The 'you' that's underneath the weight is finally breathing."

Adelita gives me a handful of seconds to digest the wisdom, and then leads me through a second breath. Then another.

By the fifth long inhale and exhale, I'm so relaxed, my limbs feel fresh from a massage. I blink at my arms, shocked at how light I feel.

"I'm proud of you, Rafael." She leans up on her toes and pecks my lips. I love how seamless our harmless flirtation feels. Her kiss reminds me that, even though I'm standing behind what looks like a haven for rats and bad drug deals, I am in a safe place with her.

And she is my haven.

"I love you with all my heart," she tells me, sweetheart that she is.

I kiss her once more. "I love you with all my farts."

We share a giggle before Adelita moves out of my arms, smiling at my relaxed state. "I'm going to go stand over where I'm supposed to be. I can't wait to see the new part of you when you pick up your shifter abilities and put them on." She holds up her finger. "Remember, your dragon is part of you only when you pick it up. You decide what you carry."

I square my feet as I mentally prepare to identify as a dragon, even if only for this brief period. I'm trying it on, seeing how it fits. It's not going to change the fundamental things about me. I'll still be fun. I'll still think I'm funny. I'll still be a good dancer.

Being a shifter changes none of those things.

My gaze locks in on Cruz. He nods, reminding me that he is here, and he will always have my back—even when it's covered in scales.

I press into the part of me I try never to let out of the bag unless it's an extreme emergency. I'm still torn between grateful she set me free, and scared because what am I supposed to do now with a full-blown dragon on my hands?

My fingers lose the hair on the back of my knuckles, and everything brushes with an olive hue, like someone swept me with a very specific color of paint, and then dipped the tips of the scales in gold. My fingers elongate and my nails turn to claws. My arms puff with new muscle I have yet to learn how to use. Scales continue to trip out over my entire body, giving me a slight tickle.

Maybe one day this will all be a pleasant sensation. Maybe I will enjoy being my dragon if I stop condemning him straight out of the gate. I don't want to have this divide inside of myself, but here it is. It's not natural to even lift my arm. Everything feels weighted and too long.

My stomach drops as my legs elongate, and suddenly I'm thrust three stories up. The urge to panic or curl into a ball is strong, but I'm afraid I'll crush my friends with the slightest movement. They are staring up at me with varying expressions of planning and panic, stepping backward because none of us knows what we're doing.

Man, this is lonely. Santos is a shifter, but at least his wolf can blend into the background without causing too much a stir. This… this is hard.

I don't dare take a step. I'm afraid to move at all. Cruz was right. I need to just get used to being comfortable in this new skin.

In my own skin.

Cruz is calling up to me, saying… something. My vision is coated in a film of pink. It was red last time. I wonder if that's because I was in battle-mode. Right now, the pink haze gives me a veil of distance. I have to work extra hard to decipher what Cruz is saying.

It's then I realize that I am in my right mind. I want to hear Cruz, and I'm starting to catch a few sentences.

Maybe this breathing thing actually works.

The lengthy inhales and exhales keep my mind present, so I actually am convinced that this dragon is part of me, instead of something that is entirely other.

When I am certain it's safe, I sit down, scrambling to

figure out the mechanics of just how this animal functions. The slower I move, the better I do at operating one lever at a time—one limb at a time.

I can't hear much of anything. Or maybe I could if I tried, but the work of operating this new body is so consuming that I cannot access sound at the moment.

Santos signs quickly, but even through the pink haze, I'm able to make out enough nuances to hear him when I really focus. *"Are you okay?"* Santos asks me, his brows knit together.

I open my mouth, but smoke billows out when I try to reply. Instead, I sign clumsily that yes, I think I'm adjusting.

Santos covers his mouth in astonishment, and I can make out the shape of Cruz's mouth as he swears. Adelita's smile is filled with adoration, as if her heart is so full, her chest can barely contain it.

I move slowly, extending my palm and sliding it along the concrete, inviting them to come nearer.

Cruz steps backward, and Santos pretends he doesn't understand what I want.

I'm asking them to trust me, to not be afraid of me.

Adelita beelines for my hand. I hope she'll touch my huge fingers to connect herself to me in some way. For her to let me know she understands I am still me.

Instead, she climbs through two of my fingers and sits squarely in the well of my palm, beaming up at me as if there is no place she would rather be. My palm is as large as a swing, and cradles her easily.

Cruz and Santos protest with matching panic, and Cruz even makes a grab for her.

I lift my arm too quickly at first, but then slow my movement, and more fluidly raise her up to the level of my face. She holds fast to my thumb, but she's grinning from ear to ear. She's got the kind of fear you'd see from a person enjoying a rollercoaster ride.

I don't notice how long my snout is until she reaches out and strokes it, letting me know she trusts me.

She sees me, even through my scales…

…because after all I've been through, I am still me.

7

LURKING IN THE FOREST
CRUZ

It takes a lot to really shake me, or at least, it used to. Now, I'm fairly certain a feather could knock me over. So many things are changing all at once that I'm barely keeping up. Rafi let his dragon out three days ago already, but I'm still on edge about it. Seeing Adelita cradled in his hand like that? My stomach still knots when I picture it. She thinks it's all a fun game, but he could have dropped her. He could have squished her. He could have exhaled flames on her by accident.

None of those things happened, but the possibility was there, and she ignored it.

Now we're half an hour out from Santos' curse tree, and I'm still obsessing about it, even though nothing bad happened at all.

Well, not nothing. Rafi's dragon claw tore the back of her shirt when she dismounted.

It could have shredded her skin.

That led to Santos doing his version of shouting at Rafi for being careless. The next day, Adelita bought a nail file so she can give him a manicure when we have time to bring Rafi's dragon out again.

I mean, honestly.

Santos and Adelita are in the backseat, all cuddly and cutesy. I don't want to stop that, I don't think, but I want them to smarten up. "We're coming up to Santos' curse tree soon. When we get there, we need to identify which axe is for Santos' curse, and which is for anyone else."

"I don't understand. Wouldn't I lift other people's curses if I could? Why can't I just take out all the axes while I'm there?"

"Because some curses need to stay where they are. Not every curse is in there for a bad reason. Some are keeping the world safe. Máximo, for instance, has a curse that needs to stay in place. So before we yank something out at random, we need to examine the handle's etchings. Usually that tells the story." I wink at her, then immediately regret the gesture. Too familiar. "I wouldn't have let you pull out those other axes if I didn't know they should have been removed. The other curse axes we'll come across, I don't know them all, so better safe than sorry."

"Máximo's curse is that whatever he wants will always be just out of his reach," she recites.

"I see you're aiming for that gold star. Good memory, Addy. But you don't have to worry about Máximo's axe. His curse tree is on his island with him. He is protecting it."

"He doesn't want his curse lifted?" she asks, wrinkling her nose.

"Oh, he wants that more than anything. Legend has it that, back in the day, Máximo broke off the peninsula where his curse axe was stuck, and created an island so he could try unnatural means to dislodge it. He still holds the hope that one day, someone will come along who can un-curse him."

Rafi turns in his seat. "Which is why we didn't tell anyone

in the village that you removed those other curse axes. If Máximo knows you can pull out his axe, he won't rest until he gets you on the island."

Adelita shrinks in Santos' arms. "So when we get to Santos' tree, first we need to figure out which axe is Santos', and then we have to make sure no one is around to see me pull it out. Is that right?"

I nod once, thumbing the leather of the steering wheel. "That's perfect. Two gold stars."

"How can I tell whose axe belongs to whom?"

Santos signs the answer, and Rafi interprets. "There's always an etching in the handle, specifying what the curse is in a picture."

"And after it's pulled out, then what? Do we melt them down? Burn the axes? How do we make sure no one curses Santos again?"

I take this one. "Once the axe is pulled out, the curse loses its magic. It's just an axe after that, and Santos is free."

I don't speak like that ever. I don't want to tease Santos with the prospect of getting his voice back unless it's a sure thing. But I've seen Adelita rip several curse axes from a tree before, so I let myself hope something good will happen for my brother.

Life has already been too cruel to cheat him out of this, especially now that we are so close to the finish line.

When I pull up to the forest where I know Santos' axe is stuck, I don't get out immediately. "Santos, the Kalku were wrong to take your voice away from you. They were wrong to take you and Santiago in the first place. I will do whatever I can to make them pay for what they did to you. I'm just grateful it's almost over."

It's the most I'll indulge in a grand speech, but I feel the occasion warrants it. This is the biggest thing to happen to us since... well, since Santos' first kiss a couple weeks ago. Or maybe when Rafi kissed Adelita and his entire makeup changed. Or perhaps when she held my hand and chased away my eternal demon.

Since Adelita joined us, our lives have forever changed.

I'm not sure I'll ever fathom wanting to go back to the old days, before she became part of our lives.

As I open my door, I feel the air sparking with possibility I never let myself dream about out loud.

I've never heard my brother's voice, yet still we found a way to communicate. Me, who doesn't like to talk to anybody, just drove across the country for the chance to give Santos back his voice. That's how badly I want this for Santos.

On my first step, I'm confident. On the second, I realize there are no signs of wildlife, though we're walking into a thick forest filled with foliage.

On the third, I freeze. "This is wrong. Get back in the car."

My hesitation doesn't go unnoticed. An arrow whistles through the evening air and thunks straight across Santos' shoulder.

Adelita screams, but my body is moving before my brain can entertain fear. I don't tend to Santos; he can handle the blood that's blooming down his arm. Instead I track the direction the arrow came from and charge into the woods, drawing a dagger and a set of brass knuckles from my belt as I go.

An arrow zips near my temple, and I know I should fall back. I should use the car as a shelter until we know what we're up against. I need to wear my leathers all the time. Why didn't I prepare for this?

Because no one knew we were coming here. The only thing I should have prepared was a celebration (which I also failed to do). Santos has been cursed for two years. Why would anyone be guarding the tree now?

A crazed warrior barreling through the woods is apparently enough to spook even the most determined enemy, because I hear footsteps retreating. I'm sure I look deranged, but for real, what an ass. To come for us when we're this near the finish line of Santos' curse is a dick thing to do. Part of my insanity right now is indignation, I am certain.

The tree branches whip my arms and tear at my hands, but the stings only serve to fuel my resolve. I will make this person pay with their life for coming after Santos today, of all days.

I'm not sure I have ever run this fast. All my focus and energy are going into this pursuit. The matted braid of a Kalku warrior flits in my vision, and I know there will be no hesitation in me now.

It's three long strides before I tackle the brute.

They all expect to be able to out-grapple a soldier from Cáceres, but they don't understand that I am one of two men in the entire village who aren't too prideful to learn the Kalku fighting style from none other than Santos the Savage. I'm a mix of strength and agility, making it impossible for my prey to tangle himself around me and wrestle me into submission.

I give the man a few grunts of frustration when he proves harder to subdue than I was hoping. But eventually, I find my way on top, and his face finds its way into the dirt. "Who sent you? How did you know we would be here?"

It's a stupid question, because I know the Kalku thrive off of interrogation. Even torture only makes them more strong-willed.

His wicked chuckle is breathy, like he is determined to piss me off. "Wouldn't you like to know? I almost want to tell you, so you never rest again."

I don't have the patience for this. My dagger stabs into his side and tears his flesh as I twist the hilt.

My prey sucks in his admission of agony, which doesn't satisfy me at all.

"Actually, I don't really care. You wanted to find us? Well, lucky you. I'm right here. I'll be the last face you see before you die." I lean in and whisper in his ear just to make him shiver against my blade. "Are you glad you found me now?"

He gasps through his pain, but no part of me will ever relent. That they would dare take this moment away from Santos, that they would try to keep him silent when he has much to say about the world…

My knife loses its patience as I rip it out of the man's side. My conscience tugs, as it always does when I'm about to end a life. Yet when I slit his throat, my knife doesn't hesitate. If there is one thing I've learned from the Kalku via Santos, it's that hesitation is the enemy's greatest weapon.

"My face is the last you'll see before you die. I hope it haunts you in the beyond."

The gurgling sound always sickens me, but I brush it aside because there is more work to be done. I pat him down for weapons so no children come across them on a nature hike, and then turn to assess the rest of the forest. The trees aren't terribly thick this far in. I should be able to see someone if they were coming for me.

But there is nothing. There's no sound, but for the rustle coming from the quaint parking area.

I rise slowly, choosing my steps with care. When I reach the others, Adelita is upset because Santos is wounded, but honestly, it probably won't need more than a few stitches. He's more worked up about her worry than his actual injury.

Santos signs a sheepish, *Rafi thought he heard something, so he went that way. Everything okay?*

"Got the guy who shot at you. He won't be a problem anymore. But the Kalku rarely travel alone. I don't get it.

Shouldn't this be the part where the others in the wings descend, and things get hairy?"

Santos shrugs with one shoulder. *"Yeah, but I don't see anyone else."*

I motion to his injury. "Is your arm going to be a problem if you shift? Your animal's ears are keener than most. Maybe you'll be able to hear if we're truly alone, or if there are others lurking nearby."

Santos signs that he can do it, but I need to stay with Adelita.

Adelita's mouth forms a firm line. "Ho, no you don't. I'm not leaving you to go off into the woods, wounded like this."

Santos kisses her lips just once, connecting them both so intimately that I tear my eyes from the display. I'm still winded from the kill, but here they are, being sweet, as if that's what we came here to do.

After some more back and forth, Santos shifts into his wolf and limps off, looking just about as pathetic as Adelita's whimper implies.

"You baby him," I mutter, keeping my voice quiet in case we are being watched.

"Good." Her jaw is firm, her eyes still trained on the spot where Santos disappeared. "He missed that entire part of his life. From what I understand, no one cared at all if he bled." She slaps her chest. "I care."

We wait in silence, standing a few feet apart, but gradually, we inch closer together. It starts with me shifting my weight from one leg to the other, and then she leans in. Before I know it, my arm is draped around her curvy frame, and her body is tucked into my side.

"I'm not good at this," she admits.

No kidding.

But the truth is, neither am I. I'm not used to traveling with a woman I'm worried will fall into danger. It's ridiculous, because she is stronger than I am. But she's also more trusting, sweeter, and unpracticed in dust-ups with the Kalku.

I take the quiet moment to instruct her. "Hear that?"

"No."

"Exactly. That's the first thing you listen for when you're entering untilled terrain. There should be birds and squirrels. Little critters scurrying about. If you hear nothing, it's because they are smart enough not to want to be hunted. So we take a note from them and keep quiet, so we aren't the ones being hunted."

"But you ran straight into the woods. That had to have been noisy."

My neck shrinks. "Yeah, I shouldn't have done that. I lost my head. Got a little angry and reacted. I'm lucky it all worked out, but it very well might have gone south. The Kalku almost always travel in pairs, so Santos and Rafi are out searching for the other one." When she's still clinging close, I add, "There's nothing to be afraid of right now."

Her hand smooths over my sternum. "Your heart is hammering, so I know you're lying."

I keep my mouth shut, not wanting to admit that my heart is pumping hard because I just killed a man. It's not the kind of thing I should ever get worked up about, so I don't. I can't help if my internal organs aren't controlling themselves.

I thumb her hip. "This is going to be a good day, alright? Nothing is going to keep this from being anything other than a celebration. They're cruel to take away his voice like that, as if being mute would keep him from spilling their secrets. Loyalty is the only thing that keeps people from talking, and they never gave Santos any reason other than pain and fear to be loyal. For some people, that's all it takes, but he's a good man who deserves more." I grip her arm and hold her more firmly to me. "Tonight, he finally gets more."

A cry of agony hits my ears, but I don't move from the spot. My hand cups her arm, rubbing slowly to sooth her angst. I don't have to look down to know Adelita has at least one tear trailing down her cheek.

"It's not Rafi," I tell her. "I know the sounds he makes when he's in pain."

I hold her with one arm, just like that, savoring the solace that comes when a woman chooses you to be her safe place.

Rafi is breathing hard when he comes back toward us a few minutes later with the massive wolf at his heels. He holds up his finger after sucking some crimson off his lower lip. "One down. Santos said you caught the other?"

"I did. Looks like the forest is ours."

"Are you okay?" Adelita asks Rafi, finally leaving my side to migrate to his.

He hugs her tight with one arm, his grin causing her to flinch because his teeth are streaked with blood. "Never better. It was barely a fight. Santos and I took him down like it was nothing."

"You're bleeding!"

"Just a scratch. Aw, you little softy. I'm alright." But when Rafi's eyes meet mine, there's a grave hint that he's concerned about something he doesn't want to say in front of Adelita.

I know what it is, and there's no use keeping her in the dark. "What concerns me is that the Kalku knew we were coming. Only the four of us knew we were headed this way."

Adelita turns to me. "Well, us and Tio Bruno. I told him on the phone, remember? It's how he let you off the hook so we could come here."

I scoff. "Tio Bruno didn't set us up. He doesn't want Santos to be cursed any more than we do."

Adelita's words come out slow. "Has he said that?"

I open and then close my mouth, casting aside the sweetness we just shared. "Tio Bruno is my uncle. He's dedicated his entire life to keeping the tribe protected. He wouldn't contact the Kalku and tell them to ambush us." I scoff at how ridiculous the idea sounds.

But I can see the doubt firmly rooting itself in her heart. Adelita's gaze is hesitant now as she factors this new information into the puzzle. "But he's the only other one who knew we would be here."

Santos turns back into himself and signs that there must be another explanation. *"Tio Bruno hates the Kalku. He's killed many himself."*

I jerk my chin to the woods. "If everyone's good, we can drop this for now."

Rafi nods, but Adelita's suspicion has jumped onto his face, knitting his brows together. "Alright, into the woods, then. Let's sever Santos' ties to his old life once and for all."

All protest leaves her. "Lead the way."

8

CURSED

SANTOS

Rafi trots to the lead spot and Cruz takes the rear as we move further into the thick of the trees. They are protecting me, hemming me in because I matter to them.

I haven't let myself want to speak in a very long time. The first few months after I was cursed were frustrating. Learning sign as an adult is challenging. Add to that being rescued from the Kalku, my twin brother dying, and being adopted into the chief's family... I haven't had the time for hope. It's been mostly a life spent figuring out how to tread water in the deep end.

But now that we're tromping through the woods, I am very aware of how long it's been since I have spoken. For two excruciating years I haven't heard my own voice. Though the guys are always good about giving me the space to converse, there are times I forget to speak up, because I know I am never going to be loud enough to make a difference.

My upper lip is dewy, and there's a line of sweat across my forehead. Adelita holds tight to my hand. It's not me tethering her close for her own safety; it's her keeping my rubbery legs moving. My stomach churns as sudden trepidation stands all the hairs dotting my arms on end.

It's hard to swallow, hard to walk, but I slog through the motions as we trek further and further into the woods. We lost a fair amount of sunlight fighting the two Kalku scouts. Cruz thinks they were sent to fight us, but I know their rank. They were sent to watch the area. The first one should never have fired. He's no doubt younger and overzealous, anxious to prove his worth to the elders. Taking down me—their slave turned civilian—that would be noteworthy.

Had they caught me, they would drag my body back to their cave, cut off my head and put it on the spit, taking turns peeing over it.

The image forces a shudder through my body, and I nearly lose the burger I had for dinner. I'm no prize for them; I am merely a thing they lost that they would want back for no reason other than that they stole me first.

I'm nothing to them, a slave, a vessel to serve and nothing more. With Cruz and Rafi, I am a brother. I'm their right-hand warrior. Though I have a hard time owning it, I am Don José's adopted son. He has a soft spot for outcasts—turning us into people he can pretend are treasures.

I like the game, even when it feels real.

Maybe when I get my voice back, I can tell Father José out loud how much I appreciate him taking me in. Maybe he will really hear it then, rather than pinch my cheek and grin, like I'm being cute.

Maybe Rafi will like to hear me laugh out loud at his jokes. Cruz never gives volume to his amusement. Most people don't, or at best, they do a silent shoulder-shake to satisfy a laugh. But not me. If Rafi makes a joke, I will laugh aloud, no matter how stupid it is.

I'll be able to tell Adelita how she's brought me to life. I used to sing to Santiago at night when he would cry after the elders hurt him. Maybe she would like me to sing her to sleep.

My mouth tastes like rust. Did I bite through my tongue?

By the time we reach the tree peppered with a dozen axes, I feel fluish, and like I might pass out.

Adelita's concern distracts me from my angst. "Whoa. Santos, are you alright? You're sweating like crazy."

Excellent. I'm sweating all over the most amazing woman in the world.

When I try to remove my slick hand from hers, she grips tighter. "Here, let's sit you down."

I mean to sit, but instead I fall onto all fours, panting like a woman in labor. I sign with one hand, *I don't know what's wrong with me.*

"Are you coming down with something?" Cruz asks, kneeling beside Adelita and prying up my eyelids so he can study my pupils.

Rafi thumbs at my torn sleeve and rolls up the material over my gash. He sucks in air through his teeth and swears. "Poison. That arrow was dipped in something. Santos, this looks bad. It's got a greenish funk growing around the edges."

Of course, I grumble to myself. Then to the guys, I sign, *"Of course I would come this close to being uncursed and then this would happen."* I glance down at my shoulder and cringe. *"I know what this is. I need..."* My brain feels foggy, but I push through. I rattle off a short list of ingredients to the guys while Adelita stands and steps away from us. *"You have to muddle them into a paste and then shove it into my wound."*

Rafi looks like he might cry. "What is the poison going to do?"

"It's going to eat away at the muscle in my shoulder, and then sink into my bone by morning. If we get to a store and find the ingredients, I won't lose the use of my arm, but we have to go now."

I push through the fog that's rapidly taking over my brain. *"It's going to be painful, but just ignore me."*

Rafi nods and helps me to my feet. "Let's get out of here now. We can come back for the axe another day."

"No need," Adelita says, returning to us with an axe in her hand. "It's done."

Rafi and Cruz gape at the tool that's been used to lock me in a phantom prison. Beneath the fear of being poisoned, shock hits me like helium to my system.

I open my mouth to speak, but at that exact moment, my entire being begins to spasm. I collapse across the forest floor as a sensation that feels like a thousand spiders skitters through my body.

9

SANTOS' VOICE

ADELITA

We split up, despite the fact that none of us wants to. It's faster for Rafi and Cruz to run into the store and divide the list of odd ingredients between them. They dash into the building like firemen on a mission.

I stay behind with Santos in the back of the car, holding him with his torso across my lap. I can protect him if the Kalku find us. I'm itching to safeguard him against the foes that would see my brave man torn apart. I've never been one who longed for violent displays, but his curse axe doesn't leave my sight. It's my weapon right now, until Santos can wield it. I hope he uses it to cut the arms off of anyone who thought taking the life out of his left limb was a good idea.

Making an arm useless on a mute man who relies on sign language is a new level of cruel. Whatever subconscious hope I held that the Kalku might ever be redeemable is now lost. Santos is still sweating, even in unconsciousness. His breathing is syncopated and labored. I imagine him fighting even now, warding off the Kalku to keep his arm, to keep his life.

I wonder when his world won't be plagued by this much war.

I smooth the hair back from his forehead, fanning him with a takeout menu in hopes that might cool him down. He's hot to the touch, and I don't know what to do. I've never taken care of anyone before. My mom never took a day off of work, and if she was sick, she put on her best face for me. But if I was ever ill, she made a big production out of everything, holding my hand if I had the flu, cold compresses if I was feverish.

I'm no good at taking care of a person when they are sick. I need a manual, some sort of guidance. Even looking up home remedies on my phone would be a help, but that's not possible since I don't have a device of my own anymore.

When the guys come back, they are running just as quickly as they were when they left. Rafi tears open packages and starts mixing in a bowl he also bought, while Cruz peels out so violently, I bang my head on the window.

The nearest hotel takes ten excruciating minutes to find, but by the time we're there, Rafi is nearly finished with the mixture.

No one speaks the entire time, even after Cruz hastily gets the keys to a room. When he comes to the car to grab everything, he reaches for Santos.

"No. I'll carry him."

Cruz narrows his eyes at me, but then probably realizes that I am more capable than he is for the job. He nods. "I'll get our things. Room 412."

When I slide out of the car with Santos in my arms, Cruz grabs up everything else, while Rafi has the bowl of greenish-gray paste and a bag of more ingredients that have yet to be opened.

Santos is a babe in my arms as I run through the silent

hallways of the hotel behind Cruz's heavy tread. Santos isn't heavy, but he's long, so I do my best not to let his legs bang against the wall.

Cruz opens the door for us, gluing his back to the wall so I can barrel through and lay Santos out on the bed.

Rafi almost spills the bowl of paste, but manages to steady his shaking hands. He doesn't use the desk in the corner, but plops down just inside the door and rips open a container, dumping half of it into the bowl.

I really hope Rafi knows what he's doing. I pictured healer business to involve measurements and a caldron or something, not random eyeballing and frantic stirring with bits of crap sloshing over the sides of the red plastic bowl.

Cruz's face is all business after laying his hand to Santos' forehead. "We've got to get him cooled down. His body is fighting the poison, but the fever is going to cook his brain at this rate." Cruz positions himself at the foot of Santos' bed and unties his brother's boots, sliding them off his feet.

I make it my business to help with this when I see the hesitation Cruz has while he reaches for Santos' belt. It's clear he will do anything for Santos, but he really, really doesn't want to undress his brother.

My hand touches on Cruz's. "I can do the rest."

Cruz exhales out a gust of nerves. "Thanks. Down to his underwear. I'll get some ice and cool him down as best I can with that."

Cruz hurries out of the room while Rafael stirs furiously. I don't speak, lest I sever Rafael's concentration. He's wholly focused on his task, and moving as quick as he can.

I've undressed precious few men in my life, and though this is no romantic moment, I take great care with Santos, rolling off his socks, unbuckling his belt, making sure his jeans slide off with minimal disruption to his passed-out body. His shirt is trickier, but I manage to peel it off of him, cringing when I rip it off the bloodied and infected spot on the far crest of his shoulder.

I fold his clothes in a neat pile and then bring a chair to his bedside.

I don't have the right words to say, so I simply hold Santos' hand, wishing he could squeeze my fingers to reassure me that he's going to be just fine. Even if it's a lie, I want it.

My mother's lullaby slips through my lips, barely audible, but there in the air all the same.

Sleep, *baby, sleep.*
  Dream, baby, dream.
  Love, baby, love.
  My baby, mine.

Mom would know what to do. She would have the answer—all the answers. She would have known how to get Santos' fever down.

Mom would love Santos so much. She's drawn to gentle creatures, taking in wounded animals and nursing them back to health before setting them free again. She was the constant listener.

How I need her right now.

Cruz stalks back in and grabs up all the washcloths and hand towels from the bathroom. He fills them with fistfuls of ice in the center of the cloth, and then twists the four corners together. With sure and expert fingers, he sets them down near various places on Santos' body, along with one resting on his forehead.

"Pressure points," Cruz explains. "When a fever is this high, it's no good to put ice only on the forehead. He needs it all over. An ice bath will be the next step, if this doesn't work." Cruz angles his chin over his shoulder. "How's the cure coming, Rafi?"

"It's just about… It's done!" Rafi stands with the bowl and rushes to the wound on the side opposite where I've seated myself in the chair. He coats his fingers with the thick greenish-gray paste.

I expect him to smooth it over the wound, which is a good three inches long. I cover my mouth to muffle a bleat of distress when Rafi digs his fingers into the gash, pushing the paste deep enough to make me cringe.

Apparently, it's deep enough to rouse Santos, who moans with his eyes still closed.

Cruz swears, but Rafi keeps going. More and more of the paste goes in. I'm not sure how it mathematically makes sense for this much to fit inside of Santos' body. But the determined set of Rafael's mouth stills any questions I want to ask (namely, do you know what you're doing?).

Santos' mouth falls open, and a low groan pushes out from between his lips.

It's then I realize we are hearing Santos' voice for the very first time.

A tingle zips up my spine, shooting possibility and hope through my entire body. "He's making noise!"

"No kidding. Rafi's digging his way through one shoulder to the other, apparently! It's going to hurt, Addy."

Cruz's dismissive tone tells me he's freaking out too, but doesn't want to show it.

"No, Cruz. Listen! Santos is making sounds!"

Cruz's head whips to Santos' mouth right as Santos lets loose a pathetic bleat.

"It's real? You did it?" Cruz drops to his knees by the side of the bed and folds his hands like he's been suddenly struck with the urge to pray. "Santos, it's going to be okay!"

Tears slide down my cheeks. I'm not sure if I'm crying more because I'm pushed to the edge whenever Santos is in pain, or if my tears are pure joy, seeing a man who has been chained finally be released.

Rafi is merciless, which makes him the best person for the job. He shoves more and more of the antidote into Santos' wound until finally, there's only a tiny bit left. Rafael smooths the last of it over Santos' cut, spackling over the injury until it's no longer visible.

"I need Santos' healer bag," Rafael rasps. I think he's emotional for the same reasons I am. "Gotta wrap this up to trap the medicine inside. Can't have it smearing off in the night."

I dart to Santos' black leather bag, tearing it open and fishing through until I find a bit of gauze. I toss the wad to Rafael and move to close up the bag, but something catches my eye.

It's a wooden disk, like a circular segment taken from the center of a thick branch. The sides are perfectly rounded, with markings on them that look like script from a language I've never seen before. When I turn it over, it's the image on the flat of the disk that startles me. Etched into the circle is a near perfect representation of my face.

Did Santos make this? How many hidden talents does this man of mystery possess?

I run my thumb over the engraved surface, noting the inscription underneath my face. I don't know what it says, as it's written in that same language that makes no sense to me. A burning desire to decipher it surfaces.

I palm the thing and take it over toward the guys. "Cruz, can you read this?"

Cruz is holding Santos' hand, and glances over at the

distraction I offer. "Whoa. Where did you find that?"

"In Santos' healing bag." Then quickly, like a child caught sneaking a cookie, I add, "I wasn't trying to snoop."

Cruz shrugs. "It's the language of the Kalku, but I don't know it. Santos tried to teach me, but I don't have the knack for that sort of thing. The Kalku alphabet has some five hundred characters."

When I turn the image to Rafael, his eyes widen, but then he shakes his head. "I wouldn't translate it even if I could. It belongs to Santos. You can ask him about it when he wakes up."

It's as near to scolding as Rafael has ever done to me, so I take it as a directive and place the token back into Santos' bag, zipping it up.

Santos' feet tense up, his toes balling as angst rolls up his entire frame. He grits his teeth before a breathy "Ah!" comes out...

...and doesn't stop.

For the next half hour, Santos howls while we scramble to try and do anything that might help him. To watch a tower of strength and quiet power devolve into sweat and incoherent pleas for help hollows out my insides.

I fish through his bag with renewed vigor. There's the vial of pain killer, but it's more than halfway drained. "Will this help?"

Cruz runs is palm from his forehead down to his chin. "I'll try anything at this point, but it's not enough to really do more than a dent. It's not even a full vial, and he's a solid guy."

"Anything! We have to help him!"

"Okay, okay. Of course, Addy. Give it here. I know how to do it." When Cruz administers the medicine, it only calms Santos' cries to a series of defeated groans.

"He's still in pain!" I fret. When Rafael announces he's

going to take the first shower, I don't hold back. "We can't leave him like this!"

It's clear this affects Cruz as well, but he forces a stern note to his voice and a stiffness to his jaw. "Then he will learn to deal with the pain. There is nothing more we can do to help with that."

"I don't like that answer!" I can't stop wringing my hands or pacing. I haven't stopped moving since Santos started crying out with real volume.

Cruz takes in my distress and slides the chair from between the two queen beds. He does his dance of pushing the queen bedframes together, but I don't move to help. "I'm not tired."

"None of us are. But that doesn't mean we need to pace the length of the room all night long. When Rafi gets out of the shower, I'm going next, and then I'm doing what I can to wind down for the night. If the Kalku find us here, we need to be rested enough to defend our ground. Santos needs us to protect him, so that means laying down when I'm pretty sure I won't be able to sleep, either. Gotta do what's best for the whole, not just what I feel like."

It's not a chiding, I don't think. It comes across as Cruz teaching me how he does things, and what goes into making a good leader.

When Rafael emerges in pajamas, Cruz stays true to his word and goes in next to shower. He points to Santos' uninjured shoulder. "You're sleeping on this side, understood? I'm not sure if the antidote is going to eat up the poison, or if it's going to leech it out. I scrubbed my hands with the cure well enough, in case touching unopened skin might put the poison into me. I'm not taking chances with you, understood?"

I nod once. "That makes sense. I can sleep on his right side."

Rafael starts in on his nightly stretches. "Santos would never forgive himself if he accidentally got you infected. He loves you more than anything I've ever seen."

I soak his words in, swallowing hard. "His axe is in the drawer of the nightstand. We need to make sure we don't leave it behind in the morning."

"That's not going to happen. If I know Cruz, he won't budge an inch unless he's certain we absolutely have to. Santos is on the edge of losing the use of his arm. He won't want to move him unless it's an emergency. Might want to get comfortable, *viento*."

The use of my nickname lightens the burden in my chest by a noticeable degree. I can finally take in the tightness of his eyes, the firm set of his chin. "Are you alright, Rafael?"

"I'm scared, is what I am. On top of Santos being injured and me hoping I didn't mess up the cure, you were right in the car."

My nose scrunches. "About what?"

Rafael's voice lowers. "About Tio Bruno. He's the only person besides us who knew where we were going. No one else knew we were headed to the curse tree."

I sit at the base of the mattress next to Santos' feet. He groans, tugging at my heartstrings, so I massage his left foot while I ponder Rafael's concern that matches my own. "Is it possible anyone was listening in? Like, the Kalku put tracker or a listening device or whatever on my cell phone when you first found me. Could that have happened to Tio Bruno?"

Rafi shakes his head. "Not a chance someone fleeced him. He's the leak. There's no other option."

"Cruz isn't going to take this well."

Rafael chews on his lower lip. "One massive problem at a time. For now, Santos is the only thing that matters. Everything else can get in line."

I massage Santos' foot, hoping I'm wrong about Tio Bruno...

...but knowing I'm not.

10

OPENING UP

ADELITA

Though I've made my point, it's clear to me that Tio Bruno is the leak who led the Kalku to our location near the axe tree. Yet Rafael won't even entertain the possibility of any damning light shining on Tio Bruno. So we sit on at the foot of the bed, staring at each other.

Rafael's jaw stiffens. "Not a chance. However rigid Cruz is, Tio Bruno is worse. Even the hint of subterfuge sets him off. He's on top of everything. Besides, he hasn't gone out on a mission in months. I doubt a listening device would have lasted that long on him."

My head hangs. "Could you go into the bathroom and get me one of the mini bottles of lotion?"

"Sure thing." Rafael can slip into the bathroom better than I can. I don't think it would be a good idea for me to be in there, even for a second, with a naked Cruz on the other side of the shower curtain.

My stomach heats up at the thought, but I ignore it.

I waste no time rubbing lotion into Santos' feet once Rafael retrieves the tiny bottle and drops it next to me. Though I'm sure Santos' pain is so acute that he cannot feel the massage, I care for his body just the same as if he could appreciate it. I rub slowly around his ankle, then apply steady pressure as I slide my thumb up the arch along the bottom.

Rafael smirks at me. "Listen to that."

I pause, but there's no sound. "I don't hear anything but the shower."

"Exactly. Apparently all our Santos needed was a good foot massage. He's stopped moaning. Maybe he's actually getting some sleep."

My heart purrs as my gaze climbs up Santos' nearly-naked body to his angelic face. The lines of agony are gone now, and his chest is moving evenly. I set his foot down, so as not to accidentally rouse him back to that in-between space layered with pain and unconsciousness.

A softness takes over Rafael's features as he takes in the sight of me doting on Santos. "You're good for him. Good *to* him. I like to see someone appreciating Santos."

I take in the exhaustion weighting Rafael's usually chipper demeanor, and jerk my chin to the free bed that's been butted up next to Santos' spot. "Lie down. You look like you're carrying around too much weight on your shoulders."

Rafael's lost gaze focuses in on me. His worry softens around the edges as he moves to stand before me. Instead of laying down, he extends his hand.

I reach for it, but then retract. "Feet germs."

Rafael snorts once, the corner of his mouth lifting. "I don't care. Have a dance with me. Just for a minute."

My head tilts to the side. "You want to dance with me?"

"Is that really so strange? I've had a long day, and I could use something beautiful right about now." He tugs me to my feet and fixes a hand to my waist, pulling my body flush to his while he holds my other hand out to the side. "Be my something beautiful?"

His nose brushes across mine, and I'm pretty sure I will

never not adore this man who looks for the good in life when all I can see is doom.

My reply comes out a dry whisper. "I haven't danced with a man since my Quinceañera, and even then, I didn't know what I was doing."

I hold onto Rafael's bicep as he starts us in a slow turn. "Not too scary, is it?" A quiet melody hums through his lips.

"Not scary, no."

A few beats pass while we dance—two friends comforting each other in the midst of a storm on pause.

When Rafael finally speaks, I can tell it's something he's been thinking about for a while. "The village isn't going to accept me now. If word gets around that my dragon is full-blown, no way will they be okay with that. They barely tolerate me as it is."

They are big words, so I don't parse them too much. I can tell he's thought this through. "However it lands, I'm here for you. If you stay, I stay. If you go, I go."

Rafael looks down at me in wonder. Then he leans in and kisses my lips, reintroducing me to his aftershave. I cherish the closed-mouth sweetness he's always got at the ready for me. "Thank you. And when things get complicated with your two boyfriends, I'll be here for you."

I stiffen, frowning at him. "Don't joke like that. You know I'm only with Santos."

Rafael shrugs and keeps up the lazy sway of his hips. His crooked smile doesn't assure me one bit. "Tell yourself that as long as you need to. Santos doesn't care. It's his two loves he gets to be near, so he's good. And Cruz doesn't have the capacity for a full-time girlfriend. It's going to work out. But for the moments when it gets strange or rocky, I'm here. Where you go, I go."

I nearly chew a tear into my lower lip, holding back

protests that only sound juvenile. I couldn't work any of them out anyway, because the shower turns off. If Cruz overhears this foolishness, it will not go over well.

When Cruz comes out, Rafael ends our dance, pressing his lips to the back of my hand, as if he could ever pose as a true gentleman. I love him for the mischievous scoundrel he is.

I keep my gaze from Cruz as I dart into the shower. I rinse off the worry, the insinuations and the puzzle pieces that don't add up. Every uncertain thing washes down the drain.

After my hair is blow-dried, my teeth are brushed, and I'm in my pajamas, I cannot justify stalling any longer.

When I come out of the bathroom, Santos is still silently asleep, thank goodness, and Cruz is texting on his phone. "Rafi went downstairs to chat up the check-in girl," Cruz tells me before I can ask about Rafael's absence.

"Cool."

When Cruz sees me yawn, he puts away his device and scoots to the side so I can crawl in between him and Santos. "Come to bed, Addy."

I'm a ball of tension, but when Cruz curls his body around mine, spooning me so I can still keep an eye on Santos, a hefty portion of me relaxes in his arms. I don't mean for my spine to turn liquid the second it senses warmth from his chest, or for his outstretched arm to be the perfect pillow.

Cruz covers us with the comforter. When his hand is perfectly dowsed in darkness, his free arm curls around my waist. His thumb tucks itself under the hem of my shirt under my navel.

The touch is light, resting half on my skin and half on the band of my pajama pants. There's nothing suggestive about it, I don't think, but it's clearly intimate. My body shouldn't be this open to his, yet for reasons I refuse to quantify, a contented "mm" sound escapes me.

I want to sink into the touch, and also to stiffen against it.

I also don't like that I don't know how the Kalku found us.

"You're all in your head." Cruz's breath teases the nape of my neck. "Nothing that you're worried about can be solved right now, so do what you can to push it out of your mind."

"Easier said than done."

"Nothing's easy. Just do it."

I snort at his very Cruz-like advice. "You're an ass. Did you know that?"

"Yeah, I think I've heard that a few times."

"Well, don't be. I'm anxious."

He leans in and slides his lips behind the shell of my ear. It's not a kiss, but it sends a shiver through me all the same. "Why are you anxious, Addy?"

I indulge myself in a deep breath so I don't answer without examining my words. "I don't trust Tio Bruno," I admit, my voice quavering. "He's the only one who knew where we would be."

His thumb moves from my stomach so he can brush his fingers up and down from my hip to my ribs. Over and over his ticklish touch teases me, unwinding the parts of me I thought would always be twisted. "Anything else keeping us awake right now?"

"Santos is injured. I should stay awake until he's better."

"Solid logic. What if he's not better for days? Are you not going to sleep until then?"

I chew on my lower lip. "I'll sleep at some point. Do you think it'll really take days?"

"Nah. But you need to sleep, either way. You can't keep yourself up like this."

"Wanna bet?" I can worry myself sick if I want to.

Cruz takes hold of my wrist and brings it up to his mouth, kissing the tender flesh and turning my body into a puddle of goo. Then he places my hand atop Santos' wrist, dragging his fingers up my arm so I can get a good look at his hands making themselves at home on my body.

"Tuck on in here. I'm tired. We can fight about how worried you need to be when the sun's up."

I sink further into Cruz's arms, completely protected by this huge body that never had to learn how to be gentle, until now.

"Hey," Cruz whispers, though the only person who could overhear is Santos, who is passed clean out. "How about you don't ditch us ever again. I about lost my mind trying to find you."

I chuckle in his embrace that wholly engulfs me. "I won't."

"Good. You like it here?"

I know he's not talking about the hotel room, which is pretty standard. I know he means to ask if I like being this close to him, nestled in his arms.

My cheeks heat, and I don't know how to answer. I mean, of course I like the heavy blanket of his body partially draped across mine. Of course I like his steady heartbeat. It's easy to find when he's asleep, and can't open his mouth to argue that the organ simply doesn't exist.

But I don't know how to put those things into words, so I answer with the bare minimum confession. "I like it when you're nice to me. But most of the time, I want to push you off a cliff."

He chuckles, and I can feel his smile against the back of my head. "That's exactly right. Keep me on that short leash, and one day, I'll learn."

My eyebrows shoot up that he would ever utter something so very...

I don't know what's gotten into him, but as I relax and indulge in the smell of him, I find I don't mind it one bit.

Cruz finally drifts off to sleep, but my mind is wide awake.

11

RAFAEL'S REQUEST
ADELITA

Maybe I should have listened to Cruz. After two nights of barely sleeping, I'm officially dragging, and my temper is a little short. "Don't think you're going to be lifting that bag, Santos. I don't care how healed up you are. You're still technically on the mend, so I do the heavy lifting."

Santos' mouth pulls to the side, as if I'm being cute. "I'm really okay."

No matter how many times I hear him speak, it still stuns me.

Even so, my expression doesn't lighten. "Good. You can continue being 'really okay' all the way into the car. If you want to be useful, you can carry the bottle of water we got you to make sure you rehydrate."

Santos rolls his eyes at me, but keeps his grin about him. "This whole bottle of water? I don't know. It looks pretty heavy."

I mime laughing at his joke, and heft my bag, Santos' things and Rafael's over my shoulder.

When I hold out my hand expectantly for Cruz's bag, he

scoffs. "On what planet do you imagine I might let you carry my things? I'm not injured."

"Oh, right. Well, fine. Let's go."

Santos picks up the bottle of water, but then drops it, his face pulling with pain.

Panic shoots through me as I shed all the bags and race to his side. "I knew I shouldn't have let you carry anything! Where does it hurt? Your hand? Your bicep? Your shoulder?"

The agony Santos wore a second ago smooths out as he takes in my distress. "I really worried you? I was only joking, *mi Corazón*. Hey, take a breath. Didn't you see those push-ups I did this morning to show off for you? My arm is all better now. You all saved it from atrophy."

The sound of his voice in the air is still new, though I've had two days to get used to it. It's velvety and low, and the more I hear it, the more I want to hear it.

"You scared me," I admit, frowning up at his cuteness.

Santos thumbs at my cheek, but even that touch doesn't pacify me. I want to make sure he's not faking being well. "Lift your arm up?"

Santos complies while Rafael harrumphs at the delay.

"Wiggle your fingers?"

He does as I request, but I'm still only moderately satisfied.

Santos must sense this, because he winds his arm beneath my hips and lifts me with his bum limb, surprising a squeak from me. His grin is absolutely incorrigible, but I can't bring myself to try and take it away from him. He deserves all the happiness he can get. Now that it seems he's out of the woods as far as possibly losing the use of his arm, he can enjoy being a man with a voice.

Santos nuzzles his nose across mine. "I have never been better in my life. I will only let you carry my bag if you understand that. I know what it is to need to watch over someone. It's how I feel about you every day. So if you need to carry my bag, then that's fine. But no more worrying like this."

His hair is so pretty—silky and black without a hint of ever being greasy or unkempt. I love the way it falls to his chin when he sets me back down.

I adore his tresses even more when they brush my face as his lips caress mine.

We make our way to the car and load everything inside. It's easy to slide into Santos' arms, easy to rest against him while Cruz drives and Rafael whistles some tune I don't know. Though we were just fighting for our lives in the woods a couple days ago, today we move at our own pace, stopping at attractions and restaurants that look interesting.

Best of all, Santos gets to tell me stories.

"Santiago was the sensitive one of the two of us. He cried when we had to drink the broth from the boiled hearts."

My nose crinkles without me meaning to display my distaste. "The hearts they stole from the women they captured?"

Santos nods and then grimaces, as if only just realizing this story might not be the best one to select. "Yes. If a woman had an ability or a quality they wanted, they abducted her, threw her into the pit for three days, letting her get nice and afraid, and then they would cut her heart out when it was most active. Then they threw it into a pot of water, boiled it, and everyone in the cave drank some. The elders ate the boiled heart, of course, but they gave Santiago and I cups of the broth. 'You're only as strong as your weakest slave.'"

My whole mouth tastes bitter now, thanks to that little tidbit of non-wisdom. "They really talk like that?"

Santos smiles, as if talking about the good old days. "Oh, yes. They have loads of sayings to keep us in line. 'Early to rise, or your beating will be no surprise.' 'Sickness is for those ready to die.'"

"Had," Cruz corrects, gripping the steering wheel. "They *had* loads of sayings. You're not with them anymore. They are in the past."

Santos' mouth pulls to the side. "I guess that's true. But they still say it. Those idioms have been around for hundreds of years."

I scratch a spot on my elbow. "And Máximo is like them?"

"I'd guess so, yes. I've never met the man. He wasn't from our clan, and he's far older than I am. He was cursed before I was born, and then formed his own island. But I would imagine the teachings of the Kalku haven't changed much with time. I can't even think that far ahead to guess when they'll be gone from my memories."

My fingers twine through his, and I silently vow that I will never let Santos live in those horrors again. *We* will become the memories that never fade—all four of us. We will enjoy our lives so much that his brain won't have room enough for the teachings of the Kalku.

Starting now.

"Are the Kalku like, actively tracking us right this second?" I ask, leaning forward in my seat.

Cruz checks his mirrors. "Not to my knowledge. Why?"

"Because we haven't actually done much living, and I think it's time we did something that doesn't have to do with violence or drama. Like literally anything. Going to a movie, bowling… anything."

Cruz frowns, which is to be expected, but Rafael comes to life. My favorite dragon shifter turns in his seat. "Yes. Finally. That's two votes for fun, instead of just me holding the party torch all by my lonesome." He slaps his hands together and rubs them with a mischievous glint in his eyes. "Santos has his voice back. I vote we commemorate that with something awesome."

Santos is a whole new man, now that he can speak aloud. He's more relaxed and he doesn't seem so anxious in his own skin. "What do you have in mind?"

"Bowling isn't a celebration," Rafael rules. "And neither is going to a movie."

"We could go shooting," Cruz suggests.

Rafael rolls his eyes. "Nothing to do with work. Play by the rules, Chief Junior." Rafael pulls out his phone and starts typing in the search bar for activities to do. Not half a minute later, he's grinning at us. "If we keep heading this way, we'll be there in three hours. Perfect."

"Where?"

Rafael pockets his phone. "Not a chance. You'll find out when we get there. We're going to have fun for once. We're going to do something different. Something that has nothing to do with the village or saving lives. We're always moving, but this time, I'm putting my foot down. Fun only."

Cruz shakes his head. "What's the point?"

Rafael gapes at the driver. "What did Tio Bruno get you for your seventh birthday?"

"A knife."

"And your eighth?"

"A knife. He always gets me a knife if I've been good that year."

"That's not a gift, Cruz. It's a weapon. We need fun. We've been conditioned to only serve the tribe, like we can't exist outside of that function. I'm telling you, I need a day of fun, or I'm going to turn into you—surly and afraid of taking a day off."

Cruz groans. "I can already tell I'm going to hate this."

"Yes, you are, and I couldn't care less."

Rafael warns us not to eat too much when we stop a

couple hours later for food. He still won't tell us a thing, and doesn't say a word until the top of a roller coaster comes into view. He's practically bouncing in his seat. "I've always wanted to go to one of these!"

"Is that so?" Cruz pulls into the massive lot and pays far too much for parking, in my opinion. But Cruz never grouses about money, only the effort of wasting time or enjoying his life.

"Not a traveling fair, but a permanent park where the roller coasters are cemented into the ground. Tell me that's not epic!" Rafael points ahead to a track so high and twisted that my stomach drops at the sight.

"It's far bigger than anything I've ever seen at a fair," I admit. "Can I say I'm too old and rickety for a roller coaster?"

Rafael shakes his head. "You can say you're too scared, but it won't matter. We're going to ride everything in this stinking park, and we're not going to talk about the Kalku or anything troubling. My brother got his voice back. I think he should put it to good use screaming his guts out."

When we get into the park, the bustle of people everywhere is impressive. It's enough to keep us knit tightly together. Rafael is grinning from ear to ear, looking as precious as a little boy at his first fair. Though this is no carnival. This is a real theme park. Mom and I never had money for an extravagance like this.

Santos and Cruz hem me in, clearly not liking the fact that there are so many people around us. "This isn't safe," Santos complains. "I don't like how crowded it is here. If someone fired an arrow, there's no way we could track them down."

I stop our quick steps abruptly. "Wow. Rafael was right. We need this day. If we can't go to a theme park without thinking we're going to be attacked, then it's been too long since you've all had a break. Everyone needs to breathe. A nice, deep breath right now. I mean it."

I wait until they all comply, even Cruz, and then I fill my lungs with the sweetness of cotton candy, roasted candied nuts, and something that smells like fresh donuts.

Rafael lets out a deep, guttural groan that spooks a nearby mother. She scurries her children away from us.

I can't help but smile at how strange we are, that we need to be convinced to enjoy our lives. "Smell that? It's one day of freedom. Just one. Which roller coaster are we hitting first, Rafi?"

Rafael scoops me in his arms and twirls me around, spilling my giggles all over the concrete. "I don't know what I would do without you. It would be just me, fighting the good fight for fun. Now there's two of us." Rafi's smile beams up at me before he puts me back down. "They don't stand a chance." Then he points to the nearest massive series of looped tracks. "That one. Let's do them all. We'll start here and make our way through the park. First one who pukes has to drive the rest of the way to the hotel tonight."

The four of us trot to the line, which is uncommonly long. Cruz grumbles that such a wait is ridiculous and beneath us, but Rafael holds up his hand before Cruz can start shoving people out of the way. "We're normal civilians today. Our biggest problems are how long our lawn gets and like… I dunno, taxes or something. Whatever normal people complain about."

The wait is forty minutes long, which apparently is "really good," according to the group in front of us. "It's usually an hour and a half per ride. It's a slow day today, which means you'll be able to ride more coasters."

Cruz doesn't like the idea of anyone talking to me. He narrows his eyes at each interaction as if they could all have concealed weapons on them. Rafael made the guys leave all but the bare essentials in the car, which was no small argument.

When we get to the front, my smile is mixed with terror. I've never been in an airplane. I've never climbed a mountain. I've never been to a county fair. To be this near to the rumbling and gleeful screams is setting my nerves on edge.

I want to do this. I want to do this.

I want to be wild for a day.

I also want not to barf on my boyfriend.

Nerves take over when it's finally our turn to ride the rattling death trap. "You all go ahead. I'll catch the next one."

Santos is just as anxious. "Just how safe is this thing? How many people have died on it?"

Cruz does his part to hold up the line, interrogating the rollercoaster worker about the mechanics, asking just how many injuries have happened on this particular ride.

Rafael lets out a frustrated groan. "You three are the worst! All I wanted was one day of fun. One day to forget everything and pretend we didn't all have our childhoods snatched away."

Though I hate the prospect of riding the thing, Rafael's real pain jumps to the front of the line. The three of us duck our heads like the bad teenagers we are, and slump into the cart that's four seats wide. The conductor, or whatever he's called, makes sure we're all buckled into the harnesses (anything that needs a harness is usually a bad idea, in my opinion), and the safety bar is lowered. The guys are muscular and bulky, but I don't care that I'm squished in the middle. I'm hoping their bodies will keep mine from catapulting out of the cart and splattering on the pavement below.

A terrified noise sneaks out of me the second the contraption starts moving. We're going at a slow pace around the first corner, but then we're confronted with the tallest, steepest metal track I've ever encountered. It looks like it goes straight up in the air, and I can hear every slow click that moves us along at a snail's pace.

Unbidden, raw confessions begin to burst out of me as I grip the bar. "I stole a chocolate cupcake from the school bake sale when I was seven years old. I knew it was wrong, but I didn't have any money and I really wanted the cupcake!" As if I'm nearing my death, more confessions burble out of me. "I speed sometimes for no reason at all. I'm not driving anywhere important, and I'm not running late. I just wanted to break a law for no reason! Sometimes I pretend I don't see a homeless person on the side of the road, holding up a sign and asking for help. I'm a terrible person!"

Rafael is on Santos' other side, his arms raised like everyone else.

Not me. I'm gripping the bar, willing it to hold me in place.

Cruz laughs through his nose, which is just about the last sound I expect him to make. "What a terrible person you are. I'm not sure I want to die on this ride next to you. Rafi, let's trade seats."

"Don't you dare!" I scream. As we climb higher, my conscience purges itself in case these moments are my last. "I lied to my professor once. I told him that my computer crashed the night before my term paper was due, but it hadn't crashed! I was just overcommitted and didn't think anything through. I lied!"

Cruz cups his hands around his mouth and shouts to the people below, "Get the town elders! I've got a liar next to me!"

I would slap at Cruz, but I can't bring myself to let go of the bar. "Stop it!"

"They're going to revoke your degree for sure."

Terror zings through me. "Don't joke about that! Don't you think that haunts me still?"

At this, Cruz barks out a laugh so loud that even Rafael turns to stare. "What did I miss?"

Cruz rests his hand atop mine. "We've been traveling with the worst kind of human all this time. I bet she doesn't even recycle."

"I do so!" I huff, indignant.

Cruz's arm finds its way around my shoulders, and suddenly, he's your average rollercoaster-riding guy, enjoying his thrill. "Of course you do. Hold on tight, Addy. Here it comes!"

The peak is so high that I can't bring myself to breathe. I don't mean to grip too tight, but when I do, holding the bar in place over our laps, suddenly I hear a metallic creak and then a terrifying crack.

The bar that was horizontal over our laps is now dangling in my grip, completely useless for holding us in place.

Terror coats my insides as a scream belts out of me.

We're going to die, and I am the thing that will kill us.

12

THE LAST RIDE OF MY LIFE
ADELITA

"What was that?" Santos looks around at the sound of the metallic crack, but doesn't spot the problem.

Vomit rises in my throat as the roller coaster keeps climbing higher at its slow pace. The horizontal lap bar was supposed to keep us in place, but now it's a useless piece of scrap metal in my hands. "I... I... I broke the safety bar! I didn't mean to! I was holding on too tight and... and... we're going to die!"

Rafael hears none of this. His arms are up in the air and the biggest smile paints his face.

Cruz snaps into action. "Everyone, lean back. We have to get rid of this thing, or it's going to knock someone behind us clean out. Addy, lift it up and thread it toward me." He turns to his right and looks down. Then he turns back to me, green around the gills when confronted with how high up we are. Still, he's Cruz, so he muscles through. "There's nothing but trees on this side. The whole area is closed off to foot traffic. I'll throw it over."

I do as he requests, with Rafael finally noticing we have a

very big problem. When the metal bar flings over Cruz's side and clatters below, the sounds of maybe hundreds of people screaming that there's something wrong with the ride hits my nervous system. "We needed that pole! We're going to die!"

Rafael grips the remnants of the metal handle that's on his side of the cart. "We've still got our seatbelts on. That bar was probably just a precaution."

"Probably?!"

Rafael holds tight to Santos' hand as we climb impossibly higher. "Cruz, there's a handle on your side. Hold onto it, just in case, and keep a grip on Addy." Then, so I don't lose my mind, Rafi adds, "As a precaution."

Incoherent sobs burst out of me. Whatever a panic attack feels like, this is worse. I've bypassed a healthy purging of emotions and am wholly hysterical, quaking from head to toe.

I'm going to get my three loves killed.

Cruz doesn't hold my hand, like Rafael and Santos are doing. Instead he keeps his arm firmly wrapped around me, while Santos curves his fingers around my wrist. Cruz is scared, I can feel it in his muscle, but his voice is steady as he speaks in my ear. "I'm always watching. If I'm here, I will always keep you safe."

A sob breaks loose from my heart and cracks out into the universe. I'm utterly shaking in his arms, trembling so bad, I'm surprised I don't vibrate us clear off the track.

And just like that, we're out of time.

I look down as we glide over the top, which is my first mistake. Well, second. First was getting on this thing to begin with.

I expect to see tracks, but there's nothing. As we're dragged over the edge by the front few cars, there's the sensation of weightless floating, of falling, of not knowing where or how we'll land. My butt leaves the seat, but thankfully, the seatbelts keep us tethered in place.

We charge through the air at a speed I cannot quantify, which I'm sure is repayment for all the times I sped unnecessarily while on the road. We loop upside-down, and whip around turns so quickly; my brain can scarcely keep up.

The ride, which we were told lasts for three minutes and thirty seconds, thrusts us forward and jerks us around for an eternity. The next hill we climb isn't half as tall, and by the time we reach the top of it, I'm actually smiling. Not a pleasant, normal smile, but a maniacal grin that splits my face while I sob.

My brain has left the building.

And yet, I conquered. Granted, I didn't actually do anything but stand in line and sit in a cart. But I'm here and I did it. I rode higher than I've ever done before.

Santos grips my wrist, and presses the outside of his leg to mine, uniting us because we are going through this nightmare together.

As we near the end, the trolley jerks forward as the pace suddenly slows. Everyone in the cart either groans that it's over, or claps at a job well done. The front half of the ride have no idea what I've done.

The rollercoaster operators are shouting into their walkie-talkies, and every other cart is emptied as quick as humanly possible. Screams fill my ears, and I'm not sure if they're scared for us, or scared *of* us.

They know it was me. They must. That's why they all look so horrified.

I broke their favorite toy. I'm the freak who doesn't belong in public. I'm the woman who should only sit and listen, and never make too many waves. I did this.

The operators warn us to stay where we are, and I know

it's because I've been found out. Here, of all places, they're going to take me in.

I'm shaking so hard, I'm not sure if I've ventured into full-on convulsing.

Cruz unbuckles himself with one hand, holding tight to me. When I start confessing to my crime, he buries my sin in his chest. His hard heart can handle it, but the rest of the world isn't ready to comprehend all I can do.

"I broke it! I was holding on too hard, and when the cart jerked, I tore it from its hinges! I didn't mean to! Help me fix it! I'm so sorry!"

Cruz cups the back of my head, making sure my confession is muted in his shirt. "Keep that noise locked down, Addy. No one needs your babbling. It was a faulty ride. Things like this happen all the time."

Santos' arm curves around my waist. He leans his form over mine, settling my insides with his warmth as much as he is able. "Cruz is right. We're alive. That's what matters."

"I'm terrible at fun!" I wail. "I broke the fun for everyone else!"

Cruz's fat fingers find their way into my hair, massaging my scalp and messing my bun. "This was a cheap ride. I mean, if a puny little thing like you can break it, then it was bound to happen sooner or later."

I snort into his black t-shirt, surprised he has the wherewithal to make a joke. "I'm sorry. I'm so sorry I ruined everything!"

Rafael reaches over and squeezes my knee. "Did you eat all the cotton candy?"

"No."

"Then you didn't ruin everything."

Cruz belches and turns his head. "Oh, don't mention food. I'm a minute away from hurling all over you three."

The ride operators order us to stay in place, and then talk into their comms using short, worried half-sentences.

I can't stop crying, which is the least of my worries. I'm shaking uncontrollably, my whole body rebelling against the massive bouts of adrenaline and shame that are coursing through me. I've passed the point of demure sniffles and am all-out blubbering into Cruz's t-shirt.

When I realize this is the wrong man to fall apart to, I turn and fold myself into Santos' arms.

Though Santos is clearly shaken, his voice is steady. It's got a note of velvet to it, softening the rougher edges of life that threaten to shatter me into pieces. "It's alright, my heart."

"I could have killed you! Your body could have gone flying through the…" My sobs turn to inaudible hiccups. I could have murdered the man I…

I don't think it through, though maybe I should. "I love you, Santos. I love you so much, I wait for you to fall asleep so I can watch you breathe. Every time something good happens for you, my whole being lifts. That I put you in danger?" I shake my head, utterly losing it all over again, and in public, no less. "Please give me another chance. I'll get so much better at this. I'll be the person that keeps you safe. I won't be your downfall."

Santos lifts me easily, sliding me sideways onto his lap. Though it's a tight fit, with my feet atop Rafael's lap, somehow it works. "You love me?" He buries his face in my shoulder. "Don't you know how wasted love is on a savage like me?"

My panic probably looks savage when anger is introduced into the mix. My eyes bug and I speak through gritted teeth, aiming my wrath at the wrong person. "You are not a savage! You're the gentlest man I know. Don't say that about yourself!"

I'm being a terrible therapist. I should be an active listener. Maybe my skills don't translate to relationships.

Santos chuckles, his chest vibrating as if I've said something funny. "Fair enough." He kisses my cheek, getting my tears all over his lips. Even though I'm a ball of chaos, apparently, I'm not too messy for him.

My legs won't unlock, even as Rafael massages my calves. My limbs won't stop vibrating.

Park medics race up the steps, asking us questions and shining lights in our faces. The operator is apologizing to the rest of the people, and explaining that the ride is going to be shut down for the day.

There are minimal groans throughout the line as they exit. I think they're just relieved no one died.

I could have killed someone. I could have killed Santos.

This is what happens when I let loose.

It takes too long for Cruz's liking for the medics to check us over. "You can get that light out of my face. I think I'd know if my head fell off, or whatever it is you're checking for. We're okay. It's your ride that sucks."

They offer to help Cruz out, but he doesn't take their outstretched hands. He's too bullheaded for that.

Rafael is helped from the other side, but when one of the medics reaches for me, Santos grips me tighter, standing abruptly with me cradled in his arms. "I've got her."

He hands me to Cruz so he can get out, and for the life of me, I can't feel my legs. Cruz doesn't realize this, and sets my feet on the platform.

My legs can't hold my weight, so I collapse in a pile of limbs, awkward as a newborn fawn. I feel pathetic and stupid, clumsier than I've ever been in my life.

I fought a gigantic snake. I remember this clearly. But a mutant monster attacking me is a different fear altogether than the terror of *me* being the mutant monster.

Santos calls out my name and rushes to my side, shoving the medics out of the way with a stern set to his jaw. "I'm her healer. Only I will treat her." But when he casts around for his leather bag and realizes it isn't there, he grimaces. "Sugar. Her sugar is depleted from shock and adrenaline. Do you have anything for that?"

The medics do what they can for me, but my body isn't the problem. Or, more accurately, my body is the incurable problem.

"I could have killed you," I murmur, my eyes wide as I shiver on the concrete platform. We're a good three stories off the ground with no walls to stem the breeze, which isn't helping my anxiety one bit.

Santos' face pulls with worry, as if it's not obvious to everyone what I did. Of course the safety bar didn't randomly fall off. I'm sure every single person in the park knows that I destroyed their playtime.

Santos kneels on the other side of the two medics, who are testing my neck and wrists for damage. He presses his finger to my lips to quiet my aching conscience. "You did nothing. You're in shock. Clearly you didn't damage the ride. That's impossible." He hints with his words and his penetrating gaze that I'm not going to do anyone any good by confessing.

But that's not me. I don't want to live with a lie that big.

I turn my head to the medic, my eyes wild and the panic clear in my voice. "I did it. I ripped the bar from its hinges. I was scared on the ride, and I pulled against the bar too hard."

Rafael's forced laugh matches the compassion in the nearest medic's eyes. "It's alright, Miss. We'll get you into an ambulance in just a minute."

Cruz shakes his head, towering over us with his arms crossed over his chest. "No. Is she damaged, other than shock?"

"No, but it's procedure. All of you will be taken to the hospital to be checked out."

"We refuse," Cruz rules for the four of us. I hate it when he does that. "We're fine. You heard her doctor; she needs some sugar, and probably some tequila. Then she'll be fine."

Somehow orange juice finds me, and my muscles start to unlock. The soft cadence of Santos' voice eases my panic, but there is no cure for the guilt I know I'll carry for a while.

After probably too much back-and-forth, the crowd of official people around us finally lets us go. I feel horrible, even worse when they comp the price of our tickets and give us vouchers to a show and several meals around the park.

I want to hide under a bench, but Rafael is insistent we salvage the day.

"No more roller coasters for you," Rafael rules, "but there are loads of other things we can do." He leads the way to the standard fair games. We all take turns trying to throw rings around the necks of empty bottles.

My tosses are lackluster, and I don't even care that I miss all five shots. My free hand never leaves Santos' grip. If he minds my clingy behavior, he doesn't say anything. I'm quiet for most of the afternoon, spooked by my own shadow. I could break any of the people I see. If I'm not careful, I could crush all the bones in Santos' hand.

But I trust my boyfriend's strength. I know that he is steadfast and sturdy enough to handle being the man I walk beside.

When we approach something called the Lazy Log River, Rafael is all for it. Even though I don't see anything more harrowing than a river that goes in a loop and then out of sight around the corner, ducking through dark tunnels and whatnot, I'm still hesitant.

"I could break it," I remind them. "If I'm the least bit spooked, it could happen all over again."

Rafael points to the cartoon depiction of the ride on a sign near the line's entrance. "Those people look ready to fall asleep, which is something I think you could use. Give yourself a little time to decompress. We came here to have fun, and we are not leaving until I get my fun's worth."

Rafael asks for so little in life. Even now, he won't ride the bigger roller coasters because I can't.

Santos speaks up, which is still a surprise to me every time he does it. "I think we should split up. Cruz, you and Rafi go enjoy the bigger rides. We'll meet up with you for dinner. Pick a spot, and we'll be there at five o'clock."

We all stare at Santos, taking in this new slice of his personality wherein he wants something and says so.

I guess things really are changing.

Cruz's hesitance is no surprise. "I don't know. We should stick together." But even as he says this, he eyes one of the larger arches of the nearest roller coaster.

When Santos signs something to the guys, I pull away from him for the first time in an hour. "Hey! None of this secret talking that I don't understand. I'm still learning sign."

Rafael offers me a soft smile, ratting out his buddy because he's just that guy. "Santos was telling us that we can't be around for every second of your relationship. He will be safe with you, and he'll make sure to keep you safe, as well."

My cheeks heat that Santos was silently asking them for some alone time with me. In a normal relationship, that would be natural to assume, but the way we met and the way we came together has been so very different. It rarely occurs to me that I actually do want some time alone with Santos. Something normal for once.

Cruz gets down to business, punctuating his directives with furrowed brows and a stern line to his lips. There is no question that we will be meeting him and Rafael at the

Burger Tavern at five o'clock exactly. There is no "or else," there is only the stern command that we will.

I smirk up at him, unable to hide my amusement.

"Something funny, Addy? This is serious. I don't like my team out of my sight. Don't make me regret this."

At this, I cover my mouth to stifle a snicker. "I know. I'm sorry, it's just… I imagine this must be what it's like to have an overbearing father."

Cruz rears back, disgusted. "Is that who I am in your mind? I'm your… I'm your dad?"

At this, I cannot hold back a loud laugh. "Oh, I needed that. Thank you, Cruz. I never think of you as comical, but that was funny." Then I reach for Rafael and lean up on my toes to peck his lips. "Have a good time, and keep an eye on Cruz. He's new to fun."

Rafael grins at me. "Keep an eye on Santos. He's not as innocent as he seems."

I'm still giggling as I turn to Cruz. I mean to nod to him by way of a parting gesture, but I'm too giddy after spending so much time being afraid of myself. My arms wrap around his broad neck, and his hands fall to my waist, as if we do this dance all the time.

His words tickle my ear. "Stay with Santos. I mean it. You don't leave his sight."

"Yes, sir."

Cruz pulls back, narrowing his eyes at me. "This is a bad idea. I'll be worried the whole time."

"I'll be careful. I won't ride anything scary. I won't break anything else."

Cruz shakes his head while Santos and Rafael converse in the background. "I don't care if you tear this whole park apart. I care about you. *You're* the thing I don't want broken."

I can tell he didn't mean to let this admission slip. His

eyes widen and he steps back, shaking his head, either at me or himself, I'm not sure.

Cruz rarely knows what to do when he catches himself being sweet, and this time is no exception. "Uh, okay, then. See you at five." Then he stops himself. "Wait. You need cash."

I smirk at the cuteness of him handing me too much money. I look down at the bills and stuff half back into his palm. "This is more than enough for my allowance. Thanks, Dad."

I snicker while Cruz throws his head back at my teasing.

I migrate to Santos' side, holding his hand and showing Cruz that I'm taking his worry seriously, even through my grin. We nod to each other, and then Santos and I go toward the line for the Lazy Log ride.

Even though I don't look back, I feel Cruz watching me the whole way.

AN AFTERNOON WITH SANTOS

ADELITA

The fear of breaking yet another amusement park attraction leaves me when I scope the breadth of the ride, which actually does in fact look no more harrowing than a lazy river. Santos steps into the hollow of the log first, and then extends his hand to me.

It's not a gentlemanly act; it's more than that. It's that Santos cannot stop himself from helping the people he cares about. If it was Rafael he was getting into the log with, I am certain he would offer the same assistance. The sweet notes of his nature endear me to him, so much that when he situates himself in the rear seat of the log, I don't hesitate to cuddle up in the space between his open knees.

My spine presses to his chest, and I can feel the steadiness of his heart thumping into my back. I love the feel of his body—large but not overly bulky, hard with hints of softness, and cozy only for me.

We don't wait for the ride to start. Before the log shifts off of its underwater platform, I twist in his arms, my lips finding his.

If Santos is surprised at my advance, he doesn't show it.

Instead, he sinks into the sweetness (or more accurately, my pheromonal attack). His arms cocoon me so I can more comfortably turn in his embrace.

Our kiss barely pauses when the vessel starts drifting languidly down the river, our log floating along at a slight incline. A darkened tunnel comes and gives us just enough cover to indulge without thought of the outside world, so we take full advantage of the freedom.

I love how new Santos is to kissing. I'm the only woman he's ever kissed, so I lead him down the path gently, but with a certainty that there is always more we can explore.

Apparently, Santos had been holding back, waiting for us to be alone before he truly tasted my mouth. When my lips part, inviting his tongue to dance with mine, I can't hold back my delighted moan. His tongue teases me with light licks and flicks, tying me to him ever more securely.

His fingers tangle in my hair, messing my bun because he knows I want him infinitely more than I need a perfect hairstyle. Everything about him is exactly what I want.

When he lets my fingers slip under the hem of his black t-shirt, I swallow his gasp before his head rocks back. The smallest touches set him off, so I take my time, my fingertips dancing lightly along the ripples of his abdomen.

"I love your hands on me," he whispers, though there's no one near enough to hear us. The next log is far enough away to grant us a fair bit of privacy. "Every time you reach for me, I can't believe it's happening—that it's me you want."

We've still got a decent enough length before the end of the tunnel, so I sink down, kneeling between his legs so I can press my lips to his bare skin. It's the same line I was just tracing with my fingers, but when my lips sew small, slow kisses across the hemisphere of his abdomen, his groan gets louder as his head falls back again. He's stretched out for me, muscles tensed with pleasure only I've ever given him.

Santos in surrender is a thing of pure beauty. I love the way he practically purrs for me. His abdomen is solid muscle, and I get to play with it. The taste of him is deliciously masculine—soap and something entirely Santos. His is a body untainted by laziness or life's pleasures.

Before we reach the sunlight, I lick a long line across his lower belly, just above the waist of his jeans. He shouts through the heady desire just before the sun hits us. I'm careful to cover his bare skin, but there's no concealing the winded look of need on his face as the speed of the lazy river picks up.

The things I would do to his body if we were truly alone.

But we're not, so when he mildly recovers and sits upright, his lips find mine in a more demure fashion. However, the scandals he murmurs between kisses makes me wish this entire ride was a series of tunnels. "Do you like kissing my body?"

"Yes," I breathe. "So much."

"And you like licking my body?"

"Yes, Santos. I need it." I don't know where my words are coming from. I was never into sexy talk with the previous guys I dated. But I so long to hear Santos speak that I can't help but encourage more of whatever he'll tell me. "I love the way you taste."

He shudders, sucking on my lower lip.

I'm so engrossed that I don't register the faster pace at which our log is moving. The thing jerks to the right, and suddenly, I'm no longer able to tune out all voices except for Santos'. Gleeful squealing hits my ears, so I turn in Santos' arms, stiffening when I see the rapids ahead.

"Easy," Santos urges, pulling me closer and wrapping me in his arms. He traps my hips between his thighs, so I don't jostle too much. "We're completely safe. See that? It's just a few twists and turns up there to make us feel like we're in open water. But we're not, Adelita. We're in the lazy river."

It's nothing compared to the harrowing nature of the roller coaster, but my body still stiffens, my back gluing itself to his chest. "Completely safe," I repeat. "You're right. I was just expecting the first part of the ride to be the whole ride. But this is nice. It's good." I'm trying to convince myself as the speed picks up yet again.

I can now see why people were squealing, as the same pathetic sound escapes me when we head straight for a boulder, and barely miss crashing into it.

Santos' left leg twists to curl across my lap, trapping me to him so there's no hint of me being tossed into the rapids.

The water sprays up from the side and splashes into the log, soaking us while Santos laughs.

This is fun. This is supposed to be fun.

When did I forget how to have fun?

I force a smile to my face and grip my thighs, reminding myself that I cannot break anything if I don't touch it.

Our log races toward... nothing. There's no more water where we're headed, only a cliff that dives who knows how far.

"Santos? Santos?" I back into him, edging my whole body away from the direction of doom.

This is safe. This is how the ride is supposed to go. I'm being a big baby, and my boyfriend is watching the whole thing. He's a warrior, and I can't handle a little theme park ride.

I will get better at this.

At least, I hope I will.

14

PICTURE PERFECT
ADELITA

trap my scream behind my lips as our log tips over the edge. It's a good three stories we fall, and land with a splash below. The spray hits my face as if it's laughing at my fright.

Finally, my tension dissipates. It's a rush, but other than that, it was nothing to be scared of. Living with the guys has conditioned me to think that everything will be harrowing, and the stakes are far higher than mercy will allow.

Santos' hand smooths over my face, being so conscientious as to wipe the droplets from my lashes so they don't bother me too badly. At his touch, I remember that I am safe.

Fun isn't anything I need to fear.

I stop myself short at that revelation. It's been so very long since fun was a value I held as important. I'm not sure I even know how to go about enjoying myself without watching for a shadow over my shoulder, or worrying that I might break something important—like a person.

I remember dancing in the kitchen with my mom, making a mess and laughing because flour smudges on our faces were ridiculous, and so were we.

Without her, I started cowering away from people, afraid I might break them with a hug.

When we float to the end of the ride and the workers help us out, Santos starts signing to me, and then stops short. "I keep forgetting that I can talk out loud." He smiles and shakes his head at himself as we make our way to the steps that lead downward. "Are you alright?"

I take stock of my faculties before answering. "You know, I think I am." My gaze locks in on his, and more thoughts come to me. "I think I'm too serious. That's not who I want to be—always afraid of my own strength. I didn't used to be like this."

When we reach the ground, Santos threads his fingers through mine as we walk. "I wouldn't guess fear would be part of the equation when you've got that kind of muscle."

I like walking beside Santos. We look so normal—holding hands through an amusement park.

"I hid from my strength so much that I never really learned how to use it, or how to be comfortable with it. Maybe I need to work on that, so I don't fall apart whenever I'm confronted with it." I swallow hard. "My mom kept me calm. I think I introverted too hard when she died."

When I shiver, Santos pauses our walk. He jerks his head to the nearby bathrooms after he tugs his shirt over his head. "Take this into the bathroom and change. Your shirt is soaked."

"What are you going to wear? I don't think they let people walk around shirtless."

He shrugs. "I'll take yours."

I snigger at his sweetness. "But then you'll be wet."

He lifts an eyebrow, as if to say, "so?"

My gaze falls to his naked torso, and I'm fairly certain there's never been a prettier sight. I should remind him to put his shirt back on, but I can't remember how to form simple words. I love the dark tint of his skin, and desperately want to see more of it. Santos is the perfect combination of shirtless and selfless, which is a heady mix. It's dangerous for any woman who's trying to keep a sane head on her shoulders.

Screw sanity.

I clear the gap between us, smearing my sopping shirt to his bare chest when my lips connect to his. Santos drops his shirt so he can wrap his arms around me. I love that he does that—holding me close while I attack his mouth with mine. My fingers wind in his hair, gripping and grabbing because finally we have an ounce of space from the guys. Though we're off the path most are traveling, we're not exactly invisible.

But oh, if we were. If we had just a small window of actual privacy, the things I would do with Santos. He holds me as if I'm precious. No matter how much of me he collects in his grip, it's clear he always wants more.

And so do I.

"Is there somewhere we can go?" I ask between kisses. "Somewhere less public?"

Santos slows our kiss until it's mere pitters and patters of affection, peppering my lips with love we cannot pretend we're capable of resisting anymore. "I love you. I'm in love with you. If I haven't said it before, I want you to hear it now. Adelita, there will never be anyone else but you. Whatever you want, it's yours. I'll share you with Cruz, no problem. I'll take care of any need you have."

I still at his declaration and step back, touching my lips that still sting of his touch. "Share me with Cruz? Is that what you think I want?"

As soon as the words hit the air, I realize how obviously I must have led him to this conclusion. But I don't want Cruz. Not in the same way I long for Santos. Cruz is...

I'm not about to finish that thought.

Santos studies the sudden gap between us curiously. "Is that not right? Did I say something wrong?"

I glance around, stunned speechless at how I landed myself in this position. I want to argue, but everything that comes to my mind sounds like childish denial.

People are moving past us as if nothing at all is strange, as if a whole other dimension of our relationship hasn't opened up to display itself for the world to mock.

This is not how I saw our kiss going.

"I don't love Cruz like I love you," I finally say. It's the most truthful and frank I can be with myself. Anything else is too bizarre to be near, even with words.

Santos signs while he speaks, marrying his two forms of communication together. "I know that. I know it's different. Are you okay?"

Am I?

At my shiver, Santos pulls me back into a hug that blankets me from my bad choices. Entertaining anything resembling feelings for Cruz is clearly a bad choice I wasn't even aware I was making.

"Easy," he coos when my head finds its home against his shoulder. "It's all okay. You know that, right? Cruz and I share everything. This would be impossible if the two of you hated each other. That you love each other? It's what I want."

What? How can he... I don't even know if it might be something that *I* want.

The hollow answer comes back with a forlorn, "I don't know," so I cuddle tighter into Santos' embrace.

I close my eyes while Santos thumbs at my cheek.

Finally, words find me. "Right now, I hate Cruz. This was supposed to be our time together—just you and me—and somehow he's found a way to worm his way into our alone time. This sucks!"

Santos' chest vibrates with a low rumble of laughter. It used to be silent, his happiness. Now that I can hear it? Even when it comes during my moment of frustration, I still warm at the silky sound. "You're right. It's just you and me now. What do you want to do together?"

I glance around at the park, unsure which rides do what. "Can we just walk until we find something interesting? I'm not used to your voice yet, but I want to be."

"My voice? That's what's throwing you off?"

"Not throwing me off. But it's yet another part of you that's brand new to me. I want to hear more of it."

Santos' shoulders roll back as we lace our fingers together, starting off down the wide road that splits the park. There are roars of fear and happiness on either side, and I can't help but wonder if that's the life I am destined to have with the guys—equal parts fear and marveling.

"You want more of me?" Santos asks with a bashful downward tilt of his head.

"Only a lifetime more. You three know each other so well. I want to recognize the voice of the man I'm kissing."

His thumb sweeps over mine. "I love when you speak to me like I'm something incredible. I hope I never get used to it." He pecks my lips. "What do you want to know?"

"Small things. Big things." When I realize how vague that sounds, I cut to the topics I really do want to hear about. "Your life before us sounds scary. How did you deal with it all while you were in it?"

Santos and I take our walk together at a snail's pace. "I was scared, sure, but that was from birth. I didn't know a mother was supposed to be holding me. I didn't know the word Father meant something entirely different to most people on the planet. Everyone in the caves had long hair that I braided before they went into battle, but Father was bald. Every cave leader shaves his head to mark his dominance. I was in charge of shaving Father's head." His lips tighten. "I was born to be their slave, so I was. It was scary whenever Santiago and I were separated. Whenever Santiago was hurt, that was terrifying. When he was killed and I was rescued? That's when the real fear started. Everything I thought I knew about the world was suddenly wrong. Every move needed to be studied and voted on by all parts of my brain before I proceeded. Life in the cave was joyless, but fear came after my liberation. I knew that wherever I was, I was the wrong person for the job."

"What do you mean?"

"In the cave, I had a purpose. Many, actually. But being free?" He shakes his head. "It took me a long time to trust the smallest step forward. Cruz and Rafi didn't give up on me. Neither did Father José. And then you came along, looking at me like I'm amazing, when most days, I'm too afraid to make any real decision on my own."

I take in his concern, which clashes terribly with the merriment going on all around us. I love that Santos is himself, even here. "It sounds like you're frustrated with that."

His jaw ticks. "Sometimes. I want to speak up, but I don't trust my judgment. There's too much savage still in me. Too much of the free world that I still don't understand. Now that I have my voice back? I don't always know when to use it."

I let his words settle without curbing them. I don't tell him how very capable he seems to me, how much of an asset to the team he is. They are his feelings for him to grapple with, so I hold his hand through his internal struggle, instead of telling him how to deal with it all. "Knowing when to use your voice is half the battle for anybody, so you're in good company with the rest of us."

Santos smirks at me. "Being with you is incredible. I

never believed I could walk around the village with a woman, but when we go back, I want that. I want to show you my favorite tree. I think you'll like it."

"I'm sure I will." My smile can't be helped. "What else do you see us doing together?"

My gaze catches on a photo booth. I have no pictures of the two of us together.

He points in the direction I'm staring. "Whatever it is that you're looking at." He elbows me lightly. "If you want me to start speaking up, maybe that's something you should do, too. It's okay to tell me what you want."

Santos is the most considerate man I have ever met. "You're absolutely right. Can we stop here for a minute?"

"As many minutes as you like."

I love how careful he is with me, pausing to make sure a nearby group doesn't so much as brush up against us.

Santos looks at all the cartoonish depictions over the awning. "What is this place? Is it a game or a ride?"

I point to the inside of the bodega, which has a dozen booths lined up. "It's a photo booth. You go in and get your picture taken. It just dawned on me that I have no pictures of us. I think it would be nice to walk around with a little piece of us in my pocket."

Santos' hesitation is understandable. He's no doubt never seen a photo booth before. His whole world is still new.

His steps are weighted as we move to the nearest booth. Since he seems hesitant still, I tap the black curtain on the side as I pull out the wad of too much cash Cruz left with me. "You sit inside and it takes your picture. Then I do cutesy girlfriend things like keep it in my pocket, so we're never apart." I point to his concern and frown. "And to be clear, the piece of you I want in my pocket is your smile, not this dread you're wearing now."

A veil of wariness clouds his features. "You want this? This is important to you?"

I study his caution, the way he stands a foot apart from me, eyeing the quaint cubicle with uncertainty. "We don't have to do it, Santos. I didn't realize it would make you uncomfortable." I shake my head at myself. "It's a silly thing, anyway. Something teenagers do."

I'm in my twenties. I shouldn't need silly moments like this, or tokens like tiny pictures to carry around with me.

Santos sizes up my backpedaling, and then grips my fingers, tugging me into the booth while he holds his breath, like he's just taken a deep-sea dive. He stands in the booth like he is in the middle of conquering some unspoken fear, only no part of him looks triumphant.

"You sure this is okay?" I ask again, uncertain what to do when Santos is clearly frightened.

He signs to me, mouthing the words so I understand them. *"This is important to you, so this is what we're doing. How does it work? Did they do it? Did they take it? Is it over?"* He flinches, and I see once again how vastly different our worlds are.

But I'm not afraid of the divide.

Instead, I coach Santos through the newness. My hands find his shoulders, guiding him gently to sit on the bench opposite the camera. "You sit here, and we smile there. Take a few breaths. It doesn't hurt, Santos. Nothing touches you at all. Wait for me to put the money in."

Santos gapes at me. *"People pay for this?"*

I'm not sure if he's criticizing my spending or not, so I slow my knee-jerk reaction. "This is how pictures are taken at a theme park, Santos."

His hands are shaking. Guilt shoots through me as I feed the bill into the machine and position myself next to him, awaiting the countdown. I show him where to look when we're supposed to smile, but I doubt he'll be able to conjure up a believable grin. He's sweating now. I don't know if I'm doing a good thing by exposing him to this new bit of the world, or if I'm traumatizing him.

To ease us both, I turn his chin toward me, so he doesn't have to worry about the countdown or the camera. My lips touch on his, which is usually when he melts against me.

This time, however, he remains stiff and scared. When the flash brightens the inside of the booth, Santos spooks. He palms the back of my head and shoves my face into the meat of his shoulder, blocking me completely from the camera's view. A feral growl rips from his throat as he lunges toward the camera.

Suddenly, I know I'm in way over my head.

15

BURGERS AND LIES

CRUZ

I knew I shouldn't have let them go off on their own. "It's five-oh-one," I say to Rafi, who's feigning ease with the waitress. He slips her number into his pocket, collecting the trophy that makes him feel like he belongs.

In the short time we were away from Santos and Adelita, he has collected two phone numbers and indulged in a hasty make-out with a total stranger near the giant flying swings ride. He's always been quick with a smile for a new woman.

Rafi sits back in the booth, his gaze sliding across the window. We've got the spot closest to the main walkway, but I don't see Santos or Adelita. "They'll be here. Not everyone is as punctual as you, oh fearless leader."

My brows push together. "Santos is exactly as punctual as I am. What could they possibly be doing that would make them late?"

Rafi laces his fingers behind his head and grins. "You want me to guess? Because I've got some ideas. I'm guessing it has something to do with Adelita taking Santos' virtue."

I scoff at Rafi. "They wouldn't do that in an amusement park. She's not like that."

Somehow, as the words slip out of me, I can already feel they're too damning.

Judging by Rafi's widening smile, I know I'm right. "And how would you know what she's like? Do you spend a lot of time thinking about how she lets go when she's finally with the guy she wants?"

My boot connects with Rafi's shin, and I hope it leaves a mark.

Rafi grimaces, but then points to the window. "Don't be so sensitive. They're right there, and it looks like they've got all their clothes on."

The two move into the diner with their heads down, walking at too quick a clip to have enjoyed their time away. Santos slides into the booth beside me, and Adelita takes the spot beside Rafi.

"How was your afternoon?" Rafi asks, his arm lowering to drape lazily around Addy's shoulders.

"I don't want to talk about it," Addy murmurs as she picks up a menu.

Well, that's curious.

I glance to Santos for an explanation, but he's just as tightlipped about the whole thing. *"Get me whatever. I'm hitting the bathroom."*

The shocker isn't that he lets Addy out of his sight; it's the fact that he's signing again, mouthing his words as if someone's stolen his voice all over again.

Addy buries her nose in her menu, stalwartly ignoring the inquisitive looks coming from Rafi and me.

"What was that about?" Rafi asks, but she pretends she doesn't hear him, and motions for the waitress.

"Can I get the messiest burger you've got? Make that two. What are you guys getting?"

I hold up a finger. "Make that three."

Rafi mirrors my movement. "Four burgers, and bring me one of every milkshake you have."

The waitress casts a halfhearted smile, but frowns at Rafi's arm around Adelita.

Rafi remembers the number burning a hole in his pocket. "This is my sister. Can you ask the kitchen to put extra whipped cream on the milkshakes? She's had a long day."

The waitress perks right up, now that it's clear Rafi is still single. "Not a problem."

The second she leaves, Rafi pulls Adelita closer. "That okay with you? I think you being my sister is the perfect arrangement."

"I like it." Adelita speaks quickly and without an ounce of feeling, which is unlike her. She's all heart, wearing her emotions like bold colors that clash without rhyme or reason. But now she's silent and scared of her own shadow.

"What did you break?" I don't think my voice sounds harsh, but my words are enough to make her flinch.

Rafi glowers at me. "Jeez, Cruz. Give the girl a complex, why don't you?" He kisses her temple, which is usually the point where she melts into him. But this time, she remains rigid.

I rephrase my question. "What's going on?"

There, that sounded nicer.

Adelita shakes her head and doesn't say a word, other than "bathroom" when Santos returns.

The song and dance of trying to coax the truth out repeats itself when we have Santos to ourselves.

"*Nothing,*" Santos signs. "*Nothing I want to discuss. It was worth it.*"

I throw my hands up. "Well, at least you're not being cryptic. Did you lose your voice? Why are you signing?"

"I don't know. Long day. Old habits, I guess. Can we go soon? Did you ride all the rides you were hoping to?"

Now I really want to know what happened. But, as they both have all their limbs and don't look physically damaged in any way I can call out, I guess I don't have much of a right to press them on something they've made clear isn't my business. Santos would tell me if it was something dangerous.

Rafi signs back, playing into whatever has upset Santos so badly that he doesn't want to hear his own voice. "We got vouchers for the hotel here, so that's where we'll be staying. No point in paying for a place a few miles from here when this one is comped. There's supposed to be a fireworks display tonight. I was thinking of going to that."

"I might turn in early. That okay with you guys?" When I'm certain Santos is only suggesting it so he can get more time with Addy, he surprises me with a solemn, *"Can you watch Adelita? I think I need some time by myself. Think things through."*

Other men have hang-ups about hugs, but not the three of us. Sure, no one else wants to come near me, but we've been through too much to deprive each other of the essentials. My hand finds its way to Santos' head so I can kiss his temple, reminding him he's not alone, even though he's trying to be.

The milkshakes come out with extra whipped cream, but Adelita is still in the bathroom. The burgers come, but she's not here.

Rafi flirts up a storm with the waitress while I keep an eye on Santos, making sure he does more than just pick at his burger. Even the pickles Rafi plucks off his burger and hands to Santos go untouched, though usually that's his favorite part of the meal.

"I think I'm going to turn in early. Can I have the voucher? I don't feel well."

I sigh at the whole thing. I can't very well keep Santos

under my thumb his entire life, but I can't let this go unaddressed. "Not until you tell me what's going on, man. I'm sorry, but if you make me worry like this, then I get to hear why. Feel like telling me what happened?"

Santos shakes his head quickly. *"Never mind."*

This is going to be a long evening.

I'm halfway through my burger, cataloging every person who goes toward the bathrooms, when finally Addy comes back. "I'm not feeling well. Can I go wait in the car?"

I shake my head and give her the same speech I gave Santos. Maybe I'm treating them both like they're my children, but I don't care. I don't like secrets that compromise our team. The two of them can barely look at each other. We don't need that mucking up our dynamic.

After dinner, we hit the arcade. I wasn't allowed video games growing up, but on occasion, Dad would sneak us out on my birthday and take Rafi and me to an arcade. Rafi's favorite game tugs him in easily, while I peruse the area with the two lovebirds who still can't look at each other.

I stick a bill into the basketball game for two, and back up. "Play." It's a command, and they obey it as such. After I explain how it works to him, Santos and Addy robotically throw balls at the hoops, neither of them taking joy in a single basket. They're both terrible shots. I get the feeling they're trying to let the other one win.

Their silence is getting on my nerves. I keep them in my eyeline while I play a game that looks fun to me.

I can barely enjoy it. When they're upset, I feel it, too.

Rafi feels nothing but giddy as he collects his tickets, and then flits off to a bodega that sells fruity drinks.

I play game after game, but the mood is still dismal. We really are terrible at having fun.

I don't realize Rafi's drinking slushed alcohol until he's bought a new drink at three different booths, and finished them all. On the fourth, his volume is at a shout, and his gait is lax.

Excellent.

On his fifth, he starts suggesting terrible ideas. "We should get tattoos! I'll bet we can find a place close by that'll do it."

I hate that I'm always the adult, especially after Addy's earlier comment about me being the dad. I don't want to be the parent. I want to be the idiot who drinks too much and tries to do something stupid. I'm never allowed to be stupid.

Instead, I'm the one dragging us to our car, and then to our hotel room after Rafi loses his burger on one of the roller coasters. Though, to be fair, I'm not sure if the barf was from the cheap alcohol, or from the looping ride that went upside-down half a dozen times.

Rafi is practically green when I finally get us to the hotel. We could have stayed for the fireworks in a couple hours, but no one seems up for anything sparkly or happy.

Rafi beelines for the bathroom. I'm guessing he'll be in there most of the night. Serves him right.

"Anyone know what got into him?" I ask the mute twins.

Santos shrugs, but Addy turns her head. "No idea."

Well, that's clearly a lie.

What is going on with everyone?

16

SANTOS' SOUL

CRUZ

Santos changes into his pajamas in the center of the room we're all sharing. He doesn't bother to hide his body from Adelita, but he doesn't show it off, either. It's clear he just wants to get this day over with.

Since Rafi is occupying the bathroom, Adelita changes in the closet, banging around in lieu of us seeing her in various stages of undress.

Which I'm not going to think about.

"What happened, Santos? Honestly, I'm starting to get a little worried. Whatever it is, I can't help you if you don't tell me."

Santos responds by literally hiding from me, diving under the covers to avoid his problems. This from the man who's killed nearly as many of the Kalku as I have, and he's only been at it two years. Whatever is going on has him paralyzed, regressing in his speech and hiding away, as if that will make anything better.

I didn't raise Santos to be like this.

I rip the comforter off of Santos, only to find him shivering in his pajama pants and t-shirt. He's actually terrified.

Compassion threatens to soften me, so I hold tight to my authoritative brother role, even as Adelita emerges from the closet and sets her clothes down. "You can handle this, whatever it is. And if you can't, you know you're supposed to come to me."

"Cruz?" Adelita is twisting her fingers—a thing she does when she's working up to finding the right words. "Can we go for a walk?"

Santos burrows under the sheet, the coward, burying his head under the pillow.

"Sure, but only if it gets me some answers. I'm tired of this. You two are acting like children." Maybe insulting them isn't the thing to do when they are both this distraught, but honestly, enough already.

I toe on my boots while she does the same. We don't make it more than halfway down the hall when she finally cracks. "I think I did something terrible."

"Alright. Out with it. Whatever it is, I'll fix it." It's not a plea to make her feel better, it's a promise that will come with a plan.

She stops walking and turns to lean against the wall. "I asked Santos to do something I could tell he was nervous about, but I didn't walk away from it. I thought… but I was wrong. I thought it was something new, and that was all. That he was just anxious because he didn't understand how the booths work, but it wasn't that. Or, it wasn't just that. I should have suggested we do something else when I saw him hesitate, but I didn't. It's my fault, the whole thing."

I fold my arms across my chest, trying to hold back my frustration as I square my shoulders to hers. "You realize you've just told me nothing, right? I still have no idea what's going on."

She dips into the pants pocket of her flannel pajamas and pulls out a long, slim slip of glossy paper. "We got our pictures taken in one of those photo booths, and Santos freaked out. He was shaking, but he still went through with it. Then when the camera started flashing, he panicked and ripped it out of the booth."

My shoulders lower as understanding washes over me. "Ah. Oh, man. His regression makes a whole lot more sense now."

"Regression?"

"He stopped talking out loud. Did you notice? He's currently hiding under the covers."

Her head bobs. "I'm sorry, Cruz. I didn't know it would be a scary thing for him. Or, I didn't know it would be *that* scary. I thought he was just nervous because it was a new experience."

I hold out my hand, and Addy sets the slip of photos in my palm. Looking them over, I can see the events unfold as if I was there. The first one is them kissing, then it's a progression of Santos barring his teeth to the camera and attacking. The last one is his palm, reaching for the source of the horror so he can destroy it.

Sounds about right.

"I can't believe he followed you in there. Wow." I study the real fear in Santos' face. "I knew he loved you, but this is... Santos gave up his soul for you."

She balks at my dramatic phrasing, but it's actually the truth. "What are you talking about?"

"The Kalku believe that if you take a person's photograph, you siphon away a portion of their spirit. Have you ever seen Rafi or me take a picture of him?"

Her mouth screws to the side while she no doubt flips back through her memory bank. "I guess not. Santos believes that getting his picture taken steals away part of his soul? Then why would he let me take him into the booth? Why didn't he tell me no?"

I can't help but find her innocence cute as my head tilts to the side. "Do you really not understand how bad he's got it for you? We tried to warn you; this isn't just a crush, or even a really intense relationship. Santos has never kissed a woman before you came along. He's never looked twice at a woman. Then you drop into the picture, and he can't look away."

She chews on her lower lip. "Santos said he was okay sharing me with…" she pauses and then looks away before ending her sentence with a quiet, "with you. A man doesn't say something like that if he's willing to give up his soul for a woman."

My mouth drops open. Of course Santos would give her that. He knows I… and he'd never refuse me anything. He loves me too much, just like he loves Adelita too much. He'd give up his soul for her, and share the love of his life for me.

I back up until my butt hits the wall. It's all I can do to stay in the present and deal with this conversation. "Santos shouldn't have said that," I finally work out, my voice rough. "But it makes sense to me why he did. He doesn't hold anything back from the people he loves. If you want a photo, he'll hand over his soul to get it for you. If I want…" I can't even say the words. I don't know if they're true, so I'm not about to test them out now.

Adelita blinks up at me, a wild animal frozen stiff as the air sparks with possibility, marking the tension between us.

I clear my throat. "I'm responsible for Santos, and part of that means teaching him about the world. I've pushed him too far loads of times, especially in the beginning when I didn't know any better. My barometer that usually works is to measure his fear. If he's uncertain, that's one thing, but if there's real fear in his eyes, he's not ready. He and I work well together because I accept that I don't know enough about him to push him to that next level, even if it's something as simple as getting his picture taken."

She nods slowly. "That's good advice. I'm so sorry, Cruz. I broke Santos! I took away his voice. I didn't…"

Her voice catches, and I turn into a pathetic sap. Before I know it, I'm clearing the space between us and wrapping my arms around her.

I shouldn't be holding her. Yet when I try to let go, my body won't let me.

"It's alright, Addy. Santos is not broken. He's scared, is all. If you're in this, then let's go back in there. We'll ride out the night with him until he realizes he's still himself, and his soul hasn't actually gone anywhere."

She nods against my chest, and I can't help but think how very right she feels in my arms. I'm usually no good at hugging women. I save affection for Rafi and Santos. Their bodies are much different than Adelita's. She's soft and curvy and she smells like roses. It's heady, the sensation of her pressed up against me.

"Santos gave up his soul for me? I would never ask him to do that! Why would he let me compromise him so cruelly?"

My hand moves up and down across her back. I try my best to block out the knowledge that she's not wearing a bra. "Santos doesn't hold back anything when he loves. It took us the longest time to get him to stop shining our boots for us. He still treats himself like a pack mule if we don't set him straight." My hand reaches between us so I can tuck my finger under her chin and lift it. I need her to see my face. "But the next time you're afraid you screwed up, don't you dare do that hiding dance you did tonight. You tell me, no matter how bad it is. I can't be on your team if you're shutting me out. I can help you. All you have to do is let me."

Defiance shines in her eyes for a sliver of a second. "I don't like needing help. It's not how I was raised."

I keep my retort slow, drawing out each syllable as our mouths inch closer together. "I. Don't. Give. A. Shit."

I shouldn't be close enough to taste the sweetness of her breath.

So I let go of her, no matter how badly my body protests, and we turn back to the room. "Let's go."

I let us back in with the keycard, noting Rafi's retching sounds from the bathroom. I bang twice on the bathroom door. "That'll teach you to drink so much. Remember this night, Rafi. Whatever you're running from, it's officially making you sick."

His only response is a moan, and I'm guessing his middle finger.

Santos is still hiding, so I turn off the lights and toe off my boots, motioning for Adelita to get into bed as if nothing is weird.

After she crawls in, I sit on the edge of the bed, holding onto my brother's foot. "Santos, I know you're still awake. Addy told me everything. I'm sorry I wasn't there. I knew we shouldn't have split up like that. This is my fault, okay? It's not yours and it's not hers." I ignore Adelita's protest, because at the end of the day, this is *my* team. If something goes south, it's on me, end of story. "Look at me, Santos."

He won't disobey a direct order, so I try not to use them all that often. But this is important. I wait until he removes the pillow from atop his head to stare at me. "You need to speak up next time, Santos. A voice does you no good if you don't use it. Adelita doesn't know the Kalku. She doesn't know what scares you. To hurt you kills her. Do you understand that? You upset her today by letting something bad happen to yourself. Something you could have prevented by just being honest. Do not hurt her again like that."

Adelita protests that I'm going about this all wrong, but I don't listen. I'm the one who pulled Santos from the cave. I am the one who rescued him and took him in. He's my brother, and this is what he needs to understand he can't do this again.

Santos nods slowly. Then he signs with shaking hands. *"Am I different now?"*

Every time he does something like this—gets terrified of an innocuous nothing—I want to go on a murder spree and end the entire Kalku organization for messing with him like this.

Sometimes that's exactly what I do.

This time, I keep my temper reined in. "Do you love Adelita less?"

Santos' face pulls like I've said something stupid. *"Of course not."*

"Do you love Rafi and me less?"

Santos rolls his eyes, as if I'm not taking his question seriously. *"No."*

"Your soul and your heart? Same thing. If you love the same, then your soul is still intact. I guess the Kalku didn't know what they were talking about when they taught you that. Guess their souls are fragile little nothings, if they can be broken or stolen so easily." I shake my head at the whole thing, as if it's a done deal. "Guess you belong more to us than you do to them."

Santos exhales with such force that his whole body deflates.

It's not that simple. I know he hasn't completely let his suspicions go that he's lost a bit of his soul. But for tonight, at least he will be able to sleep.

Adelita studies me with palpable shock shining through, as if she's surprised I'm able to put coherent sentences together when it comes to helping my brothers. I palm her face and ease her backward, so she's laying down. Then I lift up the comforter from the floor and flutter it over the two.

I feel like a tool for sliding in on Addy's other side while they're whispering whatever making up promises they are giving each other in the dark, but when the prettiest woman tugs on my arm to wrap it around her waist, I don't hesitate to cuddle in.

No one sees this part of me because the darkness hides my secrets. Still, my movements are careful as I spoon her body, holding on to this woman who is clearly not mine.

17

CONTROLLING IS NOT CARING

CRUZ

The next few days are far lighter as we drive back to the village. By the time we reach familiar territory, Santos has his voice back, and he's cracking jokes with Rafi in the backseat, while Adelita takes shotgun beside me. It's been nice, having her by my side. I'm in such a good mood that I don't even mind when she flicks on the radio and turns on some guy singing songs about who knows what. Driving in the sunshine is a far better experience than slogging through rain or fog.

The singer's voice isn't grating or overly pushy. By the time the song ends, my shoulders are completely relaxed and my breathing is as even as it is right before I fall asleep. My imagination drifts off to the past few nights, where I've held Adelita in my arms, stroking her hip when she wakes, and even going so far as to kiss the back of her shoulder. Waking up to the smell of her midnight-colored hair is a luxury I never knew I needed. But I do, and she doesn't deprive me one bit.

"Huh. I didn't completely hate that song. Who sings it?"

Addy jerks her head in my direction. "Are you serious? That's Vincente Fernandez."

"Huh. Is that supposed to mean something to me?"

Rafi speaks up from the back. "Cruz doesn't like music. He doesn't like cotton candy, either. Once, I saw him kick a puppy!"

Adelita gasps, scandalized at what is clearly a joke.

"I didn't kick a puppy." I slow my speed as we near our exit. "But he's right about the other stuff."

The closer we get to the village, the more I feel my two worlds clashing. We've created our own dynamic, the four of us, and now we're about to go into a place that operates in one very clear way.

I'm not sure if I'm allowed to, but I take a chance and reach across the console to squeeze Addy's hand. Just as quickly, I let her go, so she doesn't have the chance to push me away. "When we get there, I'm sure Tio Bruno will have things he needs me to do. I might not be around for a while."

"What kind of things?" Her frown is stinking adorable. "I thought you were going to train me some more."

At our stops along our trek back home, I've been taking the time to teach her basic maneuvers, so she doesn't have to display her strength if she lands herself in a fight. Thanks to her shoulder finally healing properly, she's got four of the holds down. Even more impressive, the last time we stopped to train, Santos didn't have a panic attack at our sparring, because he knew she could handle it.

That's the biggest mark of progress. If Santos has faith in her strength, then he will stop hovering so much. He won't put himself in unnecessary danger, thinking she can't hold her own in a fight.

But Adelita is right; there is lots more she needs to learn before we can call her "trained". "Sparring might not be a possibility when we first get back. I've got to fill out a report on all that happened while we were away, then I've got to see whatever it is Tio Bruno wanted us to come home for, but we didn't."

She nods slowly, and I can tell she's deep in contemplation. No one likes the idea of separating less than me, but she doesn't need to be by my side for boring paperwork, or for Tio Bruno's disapproval that I didn't come home right away.

Rafi grins in the backseat. "Plus, everyone's going to want to know how you pulled the axe out of the tree and gave Santos back his voice."

My heart slams in my chest. "No. They can't know she did it. That puts a mark on her, even in the village. If they know someone with her strength is living in Cáceres? She'll never get a moment's rest. They'll ask her to do all their heavy lifting, and that's no way to live."

Her voice is small but firm. "I don't mind helping. I don't want to sit around all day and do nothing. If I can save people's backs and joints by doing some of the heavy lifting, that's no trouble."

"I will not tolerate you being used."

A territorial brute rises up in me, but I fight to keep him silent after that laying down of the law. I don't want her taken advantage of. I don't want people prying into her life. I don't want Máximo learning more about her.

I say nothing further on the subject, but my disapproval is clear.

When I pull into the driveway of our home, I can already feel my stern demeanor slipping back into place. I turn in my seat and jab my finger in her direction. "This is your home, understood? There will be no more running off. You belong with us. The three of us are your family."

She takes in my bossiness with a narrowed eye, and then hooks her finger around mine. "You don't have to talk to me like that, you know. I'll stay because you want me here, not because you order me here. I think you're letting this place mess with your mind." She motions to the world outside our car, and doggone it, she's right. The expectations of the tribe aren't something I can easily shove aside.

"You're staying."

"Even though I have a huge problem with your border walls and the archaic message they send?"

"Addy…"

Her voice is steady, and carries the weight of a command to it. "Try again. I need a good reason, not a marching order."

I swallow hard and dig deep, unsure when it was that I started allowing her to control the temperament of the group. "It scared me when you took off last time. You're my family now, so I want you to live with me." I catch my slip too late. "With us, I mean."

Then she does something she doesn't often do with me. She leans over the console and kisses my cheek. She sucks on Santos' tongue, and Rafi kisses her lips all the time, but the small glimmer of affection sticks to my soul even after she sits back in her seat. "Thank you. I can do that. See? Caring is different than controlling. Because you care, I won't scare you again."

We're supposed to go into the house, but my cheeks are hot and I know they're probably red enough for Eva to see I'm blushing like an idiot.

Rafi leans up and kisses my other cheek with wet lips, the tool. "I'll get the bags, you old romantic. I didn't know you had that kind of gentlemanly behavior in you."

I fight the urge to punch him hard.

When we tromp through the house, Roberto runs out to greet us, with Consuela juggling Mira on her hip beside him. "Cruz is back! You're back!"

I never know how to react when Roberto does this. I usually sidestep his hug and pat him on the head, but for some reason, that doesn't feel right today. So I stand stock-still while my seven-year-old half-brother crashes into me, holding onto my midsection as if he's certain that is something I will tolerate.

Which I guess I do.

"I... uh... Hey, Roberto." I pat him clumsily on the head. At least that hasn't changed. "Yep. I'm back. You been..." I don't know how to do this. "You been okay?"

Apparently, that's all he needs to hear to start rattling off just how okay he's been. Roberto runs to his room to get out his wooden short sword, plus a toy car, and then a car for me to play with, so we can be a team. He's got so much energy, I'm tired just listening to him.

I don't know how Dad and Consuela do it.

Rafi high-fives Roberto. "I'm putting our bags in the bedrooms, and then I want to play. Can you get me a car? A green one, if you have it."

"I have three green cars!"

"And one for Santos, too!" Rafi calls. "You want to play cars, *viento*?"

Adelita nods with a big grin, and suddenly, everyone's into playing with children's toys. I don't think I did this, even when I was Roberto's age. I don't remember much about being young. I was always at Tio Bruno's side, helping him however I could, and then getting into trouble with Rafi and Eva in the orchards.

Consuela laughs as Mira toddles to my leg, wraps her chubby arms around it, and then slides to sit on my boot. "Dadda," she coos up at me.

My whole body freezes. "No. I'm Cruz. I'm your half-brother, not your dad." I harrumph at Adelita's quiet giggles. "Why does everyone think I'm the parent?"

Consuela peels Mira off my leg, and before I've even seen my dad, we're all sitting in the living room, rolling cars across the hardwood floor. Apparently, Roberto's car can fly, which makes him the leader.

Ridiculous.

I open my mouth to educate him, but then snap it shut when Adelita's words come back to haunt me. *"Controlling isn't caring."* Why do I need to control his imagination?

Adelita is on all fours, somehow a natural with children, even though she grew up an only child. Santos is beside her, using sign instead of his words. Getting his voice back is his story to tell, I guess, and apparently, he's not ready to let it out.

When Eva comes in wearing one of her fluttery dresses, she greets us all and then steals Adelita after casting the guys a wiry, weird smile. Apparently, she's gone long enough without her new sister.

Santos pretends he's not anxious when his girlfriend is out of his sight. To his credit, he remains on the floor with us, racing cars across the carpet and making sure Roberto's is always the fastest.

When Dad comes in, he takes turns scooping the three of us in great bear hugs. I don't stiffen, as I always do, but instead I lean into the embrace, and even pat him on the back in return. Dad pulls back but doesn't release me, studying me as if seeing me anew. Then he brings me in for a second hug, gripping me tighter, I guess because I'm finally letting him hold me as close as he wants. I can feel him breathing, and I wonder how long I've been depriving my own father of oxygen because I was afraid of going soft. My dad and Tio Bruno are the only two people in the tribe taller than me.

In my dad's embrace, I let myself feel small and safe.

When he finally lets me go, fresh dew sparkles in his eyes. "Are you well, Cruz? It's good to have you home."

"We're all in one piece, so no complaints. How is everything in the village?"

"Nothing we can't handle. Tio Bruno mentioned you were going to see Santos' curse tree. How did that go?"

I narrow one eye at him. "Don't think I don't know you're changing the subject. What's wrong?"

Dad shakes his head. "I'm just proud of you, is all. You did something you wanted to do, instead of what you were told. I'm sure I should feel the opposite, but I don't. You are always the thing my heart needs. Tell me, did Adelita get a decent history lesson on the curse trees and their axes?"

I nod slowly, unsure how much of the truth I should tell.

Rafi takes over, thank goodness. "We decided to hit an amusement park on the way back. We rode some crazy roller coasters." He picks up Roberto by the waist and flies his gangly body through the living room, zooming him around the furniture while he narrates each loop and turn. "And then finally, I barfed all over the place. It was insane!"

I don't mention the buckets of alcohol that went into Rafi's night spent on the bathroom floor.

Santos signs that we had a great time, and I truly hope that's how he remembers it.

Roberto is now going to be obsessed with roller coasters; I can feel it.

Consuela points at me, her brows furrowed. "Who rode on the rides? Did you actually get on a roller coaster?"

I rub the nape of my neck, embarrassed that I am being put on the spot. "I rode a few, actually. Adelita only rode one with Santos, but then Rafi and I rode some more by ourselves. It was a lot of fun, actually."

Now my dad is wiping away tears, as if I've done something important, crossed some milestone. "You had fun? Cruz, I want to hear every detail. Then you're going to take me to this place, and we're going to have fun together."

"Ah, man. It's not that big a deal. You're all looking at me like I don't know how to enjoy my life."

Consuela and Dad exchange incredulous glances, as if to ask what else they were expected to think. Dad takes hold of my hand, like he's afraid of letting go. "I'm so happy, Cruz. To hear you took time to enjoy your life? I feel as if I should thank Rafi for this." He motions with his other hand, and Rafi sets down Roberto so he can hug our dad. "Thank you for turning my son into a child. He missed that step."

"I had my work cut out for me. It was a team effort. I've been working on him for ages." Then Rafi's gaze turns serious. "I need to talk with you and Consuela, Dad. In private."

Dad's shoulders lift and his jaw firms. "Of course. My office?"

My brows furrow. "What's this about?"

Rafi waves off my nosiness. "Nothing that concerns you."

Well, that's clearly a lie.

When the backdoor opens and heavy boots hit the kitchen floor, I know Tio Bruno is home.

I have to confront him about how he was the only person who knew we would be at the curse tree, and then the Kalku showed up. I also have to answer for my insubordination when I didn't come straight home, but let Adelita talk him out of forcing our plans to become his.

Tio Bruno is intimidating, as always, but today there is an extra layer of irritation with which he regards me.

I swallow hard and roll back my shoulders, gearing up to face my uncle like a man, and answer for all the fun I've had without his permission.

18

COMING CLEAN WITH MOM AND DAD

RAFAEL

I can't stop fiddling with the stuff on Dad's desk. He's got too many distractions for me to play with while I figure out how to communicate all the things I need to say.

Dad sits in his massive seat, and it's clear he's putting on his chief hat, rather than his playful dad hat. That's probably best. Consuela is in a chair at his side, her face composed with a pleasant smile in place.

When I don't speak, Dad leans forward, resting his forearms on the polished desk. "Is there something on your mind, Rafael?"

I drop his silver pen on the floor, and reach down to pick it up. Then I use it to tap a nervous rhythm on the edge of my armrest. "Lots of things, actually. Some will come out eventually, and for other secrets, eventually is coming right now."

"I can tell you're bracing yourself. Should I be doing the same?"

I nod slowly. "Probably."

"Very well."

I can't help my smile when Dad picks up another pen and taps out his own rhythm, mirroring my nerves so I'm not in this alone.

He's a good father.

"I love you, Rafael. No matter what you're scared of right now, that will never change. It's you and me always, understood?"

Emotion plucks at my resolve. I never received the same promise from my birth parents. I love this man sitting across from me—his black hair with a few silver wisps, the bulbous belly and the smile that never leaves his eyes. Though his skin is a half a shade darker than my umber, I am his kin.

"I'm grateful you adopted me," I start out, my throat dry out of nowhere. "If I haven't said that in a while, you should hear it now. Without you, I'd be out of Cáceres. I would've ended up in foster care, at best. You took me in and made me your son." Then to Consuela, I offer, "And when you came into the home, I was worried you might not want to live in a house with me, because of my time with the Kalku, but you've treated me like family from the beginning."

"Because you are my family," Consuela says, love beaming in her eyes as she leans forward. Though she's only a few years older than me, she is always my mother who loves me.

Dad stops tapping his pen. "I loved you from the moment Tio Bruno rescued you and brought you back to the village. Anyone would be crazy not to rush to make you part of their family." He holds my gaze with a weighty purpose. It's the most he'll speak out against my birth parents. It heals part of me to hear him claim me as his child.

I lower my head, ashamed. I can't push back the ick in my soul any longer. "I did something bad. Or maybe I am something bad. I can't tell the difference anymore. It's too late, but you deserve the truth."

Dad respects the silence until it stretches on too long, and I'm in danger of chickening out. "And that truth is?"

"Something happened to my dragon." I shake my head at myself, for hiding from this great man who doesn't deserve my secrecy. But I cannot bring myself to out Adelita's part in it all. "He isn't a half-dragon anymore. When I shift now, he's stories tall, breathes fire and looks, well, like a dragon."

Dad leans back in his seat and turns to the side, his hand over his mouth. "You... How did... When..."

Consuela covers her mouth. "Are you alright? Physically, right now, are you healthy? Did it hurt you to shift in this new way?"

My shoulders lose a bit of their tension. "You're a good mother. I don't feel any different, no. A little spooked, I guess. Afraid of the damage I could do, but I'm still me."

Dad leans forward. "Tell me more about your dragon."

And so I do, confessing to my father the monster I sometimes am, paired with the man I will always be. I'm not sure nature was wise to grant me a formidable weapon, but as I understand it, there are no return policies on genetic mutations.

Dad is quiet for too long. All I can hope is that he's not contemplating throwing me out of Cáceres and disowning me. "How would you like me to handle this?"

Then he does something that nearly cracks my heart in two. He reaches out and offers his hand to me.

I take it greedily—any offer of affection. "I'm so sorry, Dad. I didn't mean to. Please don't have me thrown out of Cáceres. I'm working with Cruz, Santos and Adelita to learn how to keep my dragon under control."

Consuela takes hold of my other hand, and the three of us grip each other tight while the truth rocks the parts we thought were stable.

Dad's heartbreak is plain in his eyes. "If you are cast out

of Cáceres, then I am, too. That will not happen, Rafael. Dragon or man, you are my boy. If anything, you are more valuable to Cáceres than ever."

I should exhale at his words, but I can't relax. "You know the village won't see it that way. They're afraid of anything different. There are walls built around the entire place to keep people like me out."

Consuela sandwiches both of my hands between hers. "You leave the people to us. We are your parents. This is our battle to fight, not yours. I'm sorry you've been going through this without us. I trust that changes today?"

"Yes, Ma'am."

"Your dragon is making you sincere and respectful. I'm not sure I like this beast roaming about, changing my boy into someone upstanding." Dad snorts a quick laugh, then sobers. "I will do better at making conversations like these not so difficult. No matter what changes in your life, I always want to know you."

A thousand pounds of weight lifts from my shoulders. "You're not kicking me out?"

Compassion swirls in his brown eyes. "Never. Cáceres is safe with you here? There is no chance you could lose control of your dragon and light the village on fire?"

"I'm working with Adelita and the guys to make sure that doesn't happen. My dragon isn't angry or bursting to get out. It's just tricky operating something that big. I won't train in the village, though. Hopefully, my dragon never comes out inside of Cáceres."

"Then I see no problem."

I squeeze their hands and then release them, leaning back as I scrub my palms over my face.

"Is that all?" Consuela asks, no doubt hoping to relieve Cordelia of entertaining Mira.

"Not quite. That bit was my story to tell. This next bit

isn't my story to tell, but I don't care. I'm telling you both, so you have a minute to get onboard before it all unfolds. Give you time to get your 'I'm totally cool with this' game faces on."

Dad and Consuela both groan, pretending to be the children, so I can be the father who instructs them on how the world must work.

"Smarten up, kids, because this is going to be weird. But it ends well, so keep that in mind."

I spend as few sentences as possible telling them how very much Santos loves Adelita, and that they are together, which Dad and Consuela already know.

Communicating this next part is tricky work, but it's going to go poorly if they are surprised by the twist.

"Cruz is falling for Adelita. For some reason we don't understand, she chases away La Sayona in his sleep." Before they can freak out and pepper me with questions, I press on. "We don't know how, but it's happening. Cruz sleeps like a normal person now, but only if he's next to Adelita."

When I announced I moonlight as a dragon, they handled it like pros, but this is too much for them to play it cool. "What?"

I hold up my hands. "At first, we weren't sure if it was just a one-time fluke, but turns out, it's not. If Adelita is beside him, she scares away La Sayona every single time."

Dad is over the moon, tears sparking on his cheeks. "He's free? My boy is free?"

Consuela gets to the problem first. "But Adelita and Santos are together, no? How does that work?"

I choose my words carefully. "It works because I don't make them analyze it too much. You know Santos all but worships Cruz. Well, he's got the same attachment to Adelita. If Cruz needs Adelita, he won't hold her back from him. So the three of them sleep together." I wait for them to absorb that before dropping the bomb on their heads. "Eventually, if things keep going the way they are, the three of them are going to *be* together."

The looks of shock on their faces would be comical, under any other circumstances.

I do what I can to lead them gently down the path. "Adelita loves Santos, and she's growing close to Cruz. Santos loves them both, and doesn't know enough about the world to feel territorial. He's just happy his two loves both love him, and like each other. Cruz is... he's feeling his way through this. He's not the most affectionate person. But I'm his brother, and I'm telling you—if Cruz ever loved a woman, he feels that for Adelita. Just don't make them define it all yet. He's still getting used to sleeping through the night."

I watch the uncertainty on their faces, and wonder if I've played the right angles. Consuela keeps shooting her husband looks of wariness mingled with trepidation. Dad is vacillating between tears and a moral stiffness.

All their unspoken reactions make complete sense. This is why I wanted them to have the privacy to process before having to see it unfold in real time.

I tread lightly as I drive my point home. "Adelita is the best thing that's ever happened to Cruz, and to Santos. I don't want it to get trampled on because it looks strange. If it ends, let them end it. If it blooms, let it grow."

Dad presses his palm to the table. "My son went to an amusement park. My other son ate at the table the last time he was here, because Adelita asked him to. Cruz's curse is lifted. I don't care what it looks like; whatever Adelita wants, she gets it."

Consuela threads her fingers through her husband's. "I agree. Is that why Eva ordered a new, larger bed be brought in for Cruz?"

I relax in my seat, grateful that the worst is behind us, and we're all on the same page. "Yeah. We've been pushing two queens together in hotels."

Consuela leans forward conspiratorially. "Do you think she'll bear him a son to take over the tribe someday?"

I shake my head, jabbing my finger at her. "Now that's exactly the kind of talk they can't hear right now. Adelita hasn't even kissed Cruz yet. We're a long way off from making babies. Don't push them. Just step back and let it happen." Even as I say the words, I know they are falling on deaf ears.

Consuela is already making wedding plans, I can tell. "I'll have more clothes made for Adelita. Eva ordered a few gowns, but it's not enough. And her hair, maybe she'll want a stylist? She's been on the road for a long time."

Dad is right behind her on the runaway freight train. "I've got a necklace from my great-grandmother I have been saving in case Cruz ever found a woman that La Sayona would let him keep. I'll give it to him tonight so he can present it to her."

I pinch the bridge of my nose, and then clap my hands on every third word to punctuate my point. "Rein it in, you two. Dial all that back several notches. No necklace, for sure. Wait until Cruz puts a ring on her finger before you go giving her heirlooms."

At this, Dad bursts into happy tears. "Do you think they'll get married this year?"

"You two are hopeless. Adorable, but hopeless." I stand, pointing at their wistful expressions with as much scolding as I can muster. They're so cute like this, I can barely hold onto my disapproving frown. "Nothing like marriage is even close to being discussed, and if you two put pressure on this, it'll break before it's properly begun. Think on that. The hairdresser is fine, but don't make a big production of it. A few extra outfits for Adelita are nice, but nothing more than that."

Consuela holds Dad while he blubbers on her shoulder. "Thank you, Rafael. We'll hold it together and do our part. This is such good news!"

I very much doubt they will be able to hold themselves together if Cruz so much as smiles at Adelita.

I move to the doorway, but then pause, wishing there was any way to get out of telling them this next part. "There's a problem I need to tell you about, and it needs to stay here." I wait until Dad collects himself marginally, and then level the truth plainly so there's no mistaking my words. "We told Tio Bruno over the phone that we were going to visit Santos' curse tree to show Adelita. He's the only one who knew where we were going. When we got there, two scouts attacked us."

"Did you fare alright?" Consuela asks, knowing the answer. It's not as if anyone limped in here or didn't come home at all.

"Yes, but that's not the point. Tio Bruno is the only person who knew we would be there, and the Kalku managed to get to the spot ahead of us and set up an ambush. Either they've found a way to listen in on our phone calls, or…"

The obvious conclusion doesn't dawn on either of them until I let the verdict hang in the air for ten whole seconds.

Consuela's nose scrunches. "You don't mean to say Tio Bruno tipped off the Kalku, do you? Because that's not possible."

"It's not likely," I correct her, "but it's very possible." I hold up my hands as Dad bristles. "I'm not here to accuse anyone; I'm just reporting the facts. Somehow, the Kalku knew information that only five people were aware of, and four of us didn't tell them. Cruz's phone is clear for listening apps or tracking devices, and so is his car. I checked it myself." When

I can see Dad is going the same route of denial Cruz took, I ease off the gas. "Maybe there's a listening device on Tio Bruno's phone. I have no idea. All I know is all I know. Santos nearly lost his arm because of the ambush, so whatever went down, you might want to quietly get to the bottom of it sooner rather than later."

I leave them with their jaws on the floor, unsure if I've done a service for my tribe, or if I've just torn the chief's family apart.

19

BLUE EYES
TIO BRUNO

I'm due to go to family dinner soon, but I can't help satiate my curiosity by checking in on my little prisoner once more.

I cringe that I've taken to calling her that, even in my own head. She's not a prisoner, and she's certainly not *my* anything. But being near her calms me, so until she opens her mouth and tells me to go away, I check on her as often as it suits me.

I knock on her cell door, which I shouldn't have to do. I don't have to do it, actually, but part of me insists I treat her like she's got opinions, even if she doesn't share a single one with me.

Well, that's not entirely true. She made it clear she wants to stay hidden away in this cell. I even offered to set her up in a hut in the village, but she shook her head, remaining mute but making it clear that she wanted to stay under my lock and key.

Of course, even when I knock, the woman doesn't answer. "I'm coming in," I warn her, in case she's using the toilet.

I count to ten, and then let myself in with my key.

I keep thinking I'll get used to her beauty, but I never do. If Cruz or the boys saw her, they'd say she looks like Adelita, but I see distinct differences. For one, the few years this woman has on Adelita give her a wisdom that goes beyond what most possess. Though she doesn't speak, and I still don't know her name, I would go to the mat defending her sensibility.

"Good evening. Have you given any more thought to staying in one of the huts? Not much interaction in here. Just me."

She tilts her chin down and shakes her head.

"You doing okay? I had my hands full this morning, so I couldn't get away. I don't like that you're so cooped up in here, but unless you stay with one of the soldiers in the village, this is our only option."

She nods once, as if she completely understands the arrangement and accepts its ups and downs without a fight.

"Mind if I sit?"

She doesn't hesitate. She's so lonely that she extends her arm to the chair in the corner to grant me permission to stay awhile. Parts of her lovely features light up whenever I come to visit.

No one lights up at the sight of me.

I never talk about myself to anyone, but this woman looks at me, and I can't help but get all chatty. "Long day. The boys are back, so that's good. José's always happier when his boys are home. The girl is back, too, for better or worse. She's got Santos wrapped around her finger, that's for sure." I sit back in the seat. "You sure you don't want to meet her? She's your half-sister."

Her eyes close, as if saying no pains her, but still she shakes her head.

"I don't get it. I mean, family's not always what it's cracked up to be, but you don't even want to see her?"

The woman is on her cot in the corner. She pulls up her knees, but her left one doesn't go up as far. She's nursing an injury she doesn't want to admit to me, and she won't let the healers touch her.

"Don't think I haven't noticed your limp," I tell her in a light scold. "You should let me take a look at it, Blue Eyes."

Shit. That slipped out all wrong.

"Not me, I mean. A healer." My nose scrunches. "I don't want to look at your hip."

She smirks at my flub, but shakes her head.

I've been calling her "Blue Eyes" since she came to us. Only in private, of course, but if she minds the nickname, she can tell me her real dang name, and I'll call her that.

Or maybe I'll call her Blue Eyes forever. I rather like it. And whenever I say it, her cheeks tint the softest shade of pink. I don't use the word "cute" to describe grown women, but if I did, I would admit her blush is just about the cutest thing I've ever seen.

I'm too old for this. Too old to flirt shamelessly with someone half my age. I didn't make time to flirt when I was younger. I was too busy protecting Cáceres.

But again, she seems to like it.

And apparently, I can't stop myself.

When her blush recedes, she tilts her head in my direction, as if asking if I'm alright.

"Long day," I explain. "If I hide out in here, no one can find me."

Her chest vibrates with a silent giggle. Then she holds out her hand and it drifts to the side, asking me to elaborate.

"The people who found you—the Mendez tribe—want an update on how you came to live on Máximo's island, and how you're doing now. They rescued you from

Máximo, but they have no details on him." I clear my throat. "He's your father, but other than that, we have no information on him. We can't take him down without your help."

Blue Eyes scowls at the notion of Máximo being her parent.

Can't say I blame her.

"The Mendez people are impatient. They want a world without Máximo, but I have no news for them on that front. The tribes don't exactly get along, so even though they couldn't get information out of you, they're upset that I can't, either."

She casts me a look of apology, which I believe.

"See, I think you want to tell me who you are and all you've been through. You're just not ready." I pause for her nod. That small communication—that I guessed her right— relaxes my shoulders. "I can understand that. I haven't been ready to tell my brother I've wanted to retire for years." I rarely speak candidly to anyone, but all Blue Eyes has to do is sit there with those pretty pink lips, and all my secrets come tumbling out. "José needs me to run things. He's had a hard life, what with his first wife dying, and La Sayona haunting him for years. He's happy now, and I like to think I help make that happen. If I hand off the army now?" I shake my head. "It's not the right time."

Blue Eyes tilts her head in the other direction, silently asking me when the right time is.

"I don't know when. I just know I'm tired. I want a life outside of Cáceres, but without me to keep everyone in place and protected, it's not wise for me to leave."

She holds my gaze, and I can see she truly wants that for me. There's a sadness etched into her that tells me she cares about something as silly as my happiness.

I take a chance and turn the tables on her. "Is the tracker

bothering you? I can put it on your wrist, if you'd rather. It's standard for rescues."

She inches her leg away from me and shakes her head. For some reason she likes her tracker. Usually, the rescues are itching to get the offending hard plastic off.

"Well then, what do you want?"

She hesitates for so long that I'm certain she's going to blow off my question with her silence. When her eyes mist over and a tear falls, I'm on my feet.

I made her cry. This is why I don't like to be around people. I'm not good with them. I shouldn't be around anyone.

"I'm sorry, Blue Eyes. I shouldn't have…"

But then she pats the spot on the cot beside her.

Is she… Is she inviting me to sit with her on her bed?

I swallow hard as I take her up on her request, the cot groaning with my weight. I'm too big for everything, but she doesn't seem to mind.

Not a second passes, and she angles her body toward me, cuddling into my side.

Fates, this is heaven. This is what she wants? Me? Or did she just want to be held by any warm body, isolated as she's been? Either way, I'll take it.

My arm curves around her, pulling her head to rest on my shoulder. My free hand reaches to her face and thumbs away the solitary tear before another can join. "Not while I'm around," I promise her. "If I'm here, you get one tear, and then I wipe the rest of them away. Understood? I can tolerate one. No more than that."

Her silent laughter touches my chest with a puff of air. She's easily far too young for me, but when her fingers touch on my sternum, there's a decidedly adult feel to her touch. I haven't kissed a woman in ages. Maybe a decade or more. I can't remember. I'm always so consumed with work.

I've forgotten what it's like to hold a woman in my arms and feel her weight against my chest.

I hold her just like that for as long as she lets me, stroking her silky black hair and relaxing.

It's been a long time since I've just relaxed.

"I like this," I admit in a pained whisper. It's akin to me telling this woman that I want to court her, but truthfully, I have no idea how something like that even works anymore. I'm too out of practice.

As if my words electrocuted her, Blue Eyes stiffens and then stands, backing away from the cot. She looks frightened as she points to the door.

"What? Blue Eyes, what's wrong? Did I do something to scare you?"

She shakes her head, but remains firm with her finger that I need to leave now.

"Are you sending me away?"

She nods, but I can see this choice pains her.

"I don't understand."

But she makes her wish clear when she lightly shoves me toward the exit.

My leaden feet move me out of her cell, and my key locks her inside, just how she likes it, even though my grip trembles unsteadily.

What just happened?

A BRIDE
ADELITA

*E*veryone is so nice to me. I mean, they were probably just as friendly when I stayed here before, but maybe I didn't appreciate it as much back then, because everything was so new to me. It's still new. I got lost looking for the kitchen earlier, but I'm getting the hang of things. There's a lot of bustling about in the massive one-story house, but Eva's made it clear this is our time, not theirs. She's firm in her ruling that I need a break from the guys.

She is not wrong.

Spending time with Eva is a breath of fresh air. I love the guys, but being with a woman is just plain different, and sometimes necessary. I brush out her hair while she tells me all about the latest gossip in Cáceres. Actually, it could be old gossip, and I'd never know the difference.

The two of us made a deal: we would converse as if we already knew everything about each other's backstories. Eventually the details would fill themselves in.

I'm a therapist, so I can guess most of it: privileged existence makes her feel like she owes her parents, giving them

.the right to make decisions for her future. Wanting to fly free of the nest, but stays because she's afraid of falling publicly.

It's all textbook.

So when Eva starts complaining about Silvia's subpar skills with a bow, I play along as if I'm already caught up in the details of her life. "That's so Silvia." Even though I have no idea who this Silvia person is, I pretend I do.

"I know, right? She talks up a good game, bragging how she's an amazing shot, but it's all to impress Tio Bruno—the one man who's impressed by nothing. I'll never understand why women get all hot and bothered by my ass of an uncle."

"He's a grumpy old man." That part's not a guess. I've witnessed Tio Bruno's brusque nature firsthand.

Eva giggles at the slight while I finish brushing out her wavy hair. It goes down to her shoulders, and is so very silky and pretty.

I fish through her box of ribbons and pin a few in her hair, and then curl them with an iron to give the whole thing a bit of movement.

Eva points to the two dresses she's narrowed it down to for me. "You know, you're going to have to choose sooner or later. You can't very well go to dinner in your robe."

I glance down at the lavender silk robe she got me, loving the expensive, slippery feel of the material over my bare skin. "They're so fancy, Eva. I'm not used to getting dressed up for dinner."

The clothes know they don't belong on me. It's like they can sniff out the stench of poverty, refusing to touch my body.

I don't blame them.

At that moment, a knock interrupts us. "Girls, can I come in?"

Eva grins. "Sure, Mom. We're just figuring out what to wear."

It's a true testament to the respect Eva has for her father and for her stepmother that she doesn't call Consuela by her first name, though they can't be more than five years apart.

Consuela flits into Eva's bedroom with a garment bag over her arm. "I had a few things brought in to add to your wardrobe, Adelita. Would you like to wear this tonight?"

She unsheathes a white dress that's far too formal for me to touch, let alone try on. The lace is so intricate, I'm certain it will tear if I come too near.

This dress definitely knows I'm poor.

"I… It's so beautiful."

Consuela takes that as a "yes," and beams at me. "Perfect. We're so glad you're here. Anything you need, anything at all, please tell me. I'm sure you're tired of hotel toiletries, so I filled your bathroom with the good stuff."

I sit down on the edge of the bed beside Eva, utterly over-whelmed. "Is this just how your family is? You take in people who have no home and shower them with beautiful things? I don't understand what I did to deserve the royal treatment."

Consuela lets out a throaty laugh. "You're one of us now. Anything that's mine is yours. If you don't see something you like, just ask, and we'll get it for you."

Eva echoes the sentiment by squeezing my hand. "How long until dinner?"

"As soon as you're dressed. The guys are just about to head down to the dining room. We can't wait to hear all about your adventures." Then Consuela sets the dress down across the bed and kisses Eva's forehead. When she bends to kiss my forehead, my whole body warms. "Time to get dressed, dear."

I miss my mom.

Though the illusion of choice is presented, there is no question that this is what I will be wearing to dinner.

Consuela and Eva chat about some festival coming up

while I take the dress into the bathroom and change. I wash my hands before I touch it, not trusting myself around something so pure.

The little bag of undergarments on the hook fit perfectly, which I've got to say, is a shock to me. I have a hard enough time finding something to fit in a store after trying on everything the salesperson hands me. The white strapless bra and underwear have a sheer lace over them. When I catch my appearance in the mirror, I still. I've never had a matching bra and underwear set before. The luxury is stunning. I usually can spot all my bodily imperfections, but right now, they fade into the background.

I feel myself standing taller, bolstered with more confidence than I'm usually packing. After the dress slides over my head, I cannot believe it's me who is standing in front of the full-length mirror. I look like a woman in a magazine. The white dress is low-cut, nearly giving me away. The hemline falls to mid-thigh in the front, but then dips to my calves in the back. The bodice fits like a glove—showing off my drastic curves but allowing me to breathe easily.

It's the layer of intricate white lace overtop that throws me. While the satin beneath cups my breasts, the lace accentuates them, drawing back like two curtains to reveal my showstopping cleavage.

It's then I realize Consuela and Eva are whispering. When I pick out my name, I know I need to tell them I cannot wear this dress.

I look expensive, which I am not.

I look like I've got somewhere to be, which I don't.

I look... I look like a bride.

I speak up from behind the door, pressing my fingers to the divide between us. "I don't think I can wear this, Consuela. I'm so sorry, it's just not fitting right."

I can hear the frown in her voice. "I thought I had your measurements exact. Let's see where I messed up."

I don't expect her to open up the bathroom door, nor do I anticipate the choked-up look that overtakes her as her hand flies to her chest. "It's perfect. Exactly as I imagined it."

Eva presses her lips together through a smile. "The fit is spot on, Adelita. What's wrong with it?"

I glance down, unsure how to tell them that it's not my body that doesn't fit the gown, it's me.

Can't they tell I'm poor?

But as every response I can think up seems childish, I muscle through my discomfort. "Nothing, I guess. I'm just not used to this. I've been in jeans and a t-shirt lately, and this is… different. Everyone else is going to be dressed up for dinner? This is normal?"

Both women bob their heads. Eva motions to her own dress, which, sure, is a beautiful gown, but it's nothing nearly as fancy as this. Plus, Eva looks normal in nice material.

Consuela is wearing a normal sundress that goes down to the floor, but she promises I'll fit right in. "Come and sit. We have just a few minutes to put your hair up. I have a stylist stopping by tomorrow so you two can have some pampering together. It's long overdue."

They're going to such fuss over me; I don't understand it. Consuela sits me down at Eva's vanity and runs a brush through my waves. "Such healthy hair. How would you like to wear it tonight?"

"Just a ponytail is fine, guys. I can't imagine anyone cares how nice my hair looks."

It's then that Eva crouches down in front of me while Consuela continues brushing. "You listen to me, *hermana*. It's good to treat yourself every now and then. You're used to sleeping on the road and wearing the uniform the guys all cling to as if it's their security blanket. While you are here, you get to breathe. The village is the place for you to be a person, instead of just a tool serving a purpose." Then she stands, scooping up some blush from her vanity. "Besides, I outgrew playing with dolls years ago. I rather miss the fun of it, so you get to be my new doll."

I snort at her logic and give in to her whim, sitting still until a knock lets them know they've carried on long enough.

Don José enters when Eva gives him the all clear. I expect him to tell us to hurry it up, but he stops in the doorway, his hand over his chest. "Beautiful. Consuela, you've chosen well. She is perfect. Girls, you are the thing my heart needs."

I get the sneaking suspicion I'm about to be offered up in some weird ritual where a bride has to dance around under the full moon or something.

Don José offers his hand to his wife and nods to me. "It's good to have you here, *hija*. It's clear I've been depriving my daughter by not giving her a sister her age. Cordelia doesn't care for fine dresses and such."

That makes two of us.

Actually, that's not true. I owned a couple simple dresses before I left my life, but nothing like this. If I wasn't so nervous, I might enjoy playing dress-up.

I remind myself to relax. I have choices. I can act or accept. I can tell them that I'm not wearing this, or I can accept a lovely gift without overanalyzing every detail.

I decide to accept the good grace that life is gifting me in this moment, and be grateful for the unexpected turn.

However, the looks the three of them keep giving me are laced with conspiratorial smiles. It's like they know something I don't.

When Eva steps out into the hall before me, her smile

vanishes and a sharp command cracks out of her mouth. "No! Do you hear me? Don't even think about it. All three of you, turn around and change right this instant. If I see those black t-shirts again, I'm burning them in the fireplace. You are not wild men in here." When I hear Cruz start to argue, I can already tell he's made the wrong choice. "If you don't dress for dinner tonight, then you don't eat dinner."

Then she stomps in their direction, and I can only guess she shoves them into Cruz's bedroom.

Consuela drops her husband's arm. "Get the box on your dresser, José. Hurry!"

"What's going on?" I ask Consuela warily as she whirls on me and herds me back into Eva's room.

"Eva just bought us some more time. I want to curl a few of these pieces back here. And you haven't had a manicure."

"What? I thought we had to hurry for dinner."

"Dinner will keep. Tio Bruno's always late anyway."

Of course he is. His personality type is an eight on the Enneagram. He likes to make an entrance, controlling the tenor of the room so everyone knows when he's arrived.

Ass.

As Consuela works quickly, buffing my nails as if that's a necessary thing for preparation in consuming a family meal, I try to think up the right words. "Consuela, is something going on? I wore one of Eva's dresses last time, but I thought that was just to meet the family and make a good impression. Are your dinners always this formal?"

"Not always, but we do try to make an effort to be presentable. It's special tonight because we have our boys home, and you. It's not often they're here, so we sometimes go a bit overboard." She coats my nails with sheer pink, adding a touch of class to my hands, which I've never given much thought to.

When Don José lets himself in, he sets a small box on the vanity.

"Perfect. Thank you, *mi amor*." When she opens it, a small aquamarine gem sparkles at the end of a white gold chain. "I thought this would look nice with your eyes. What do you think?"

I balk at her. "You can't give me nice jewelry!" I bury my face in my hands. "I'm missing a step. Maybe several. I'm a guest, an imposition, but you're treating me like a queen. I don't understand what's going on! If you think I'm some important person who deserves this grand treatment, you have to know that I'm not."

Consuela and José smile indulgently at me, and Consuela affixes the necklace in place. "We like having you around, and we're the royalty of the tribe. Chalk it up to our eccentricities, and let us have our fun. All you have to do is enjoy yourself while you're with us. That's all we want for our family."

Don José slides an arm around Consuela's waist, and the two smile wistfully at me, as if I am their daughter, and I've done some grand thing to be proud of.

And I'm being a jerk about the whole thing, thinking they have some ulterior motive. When I stand, shaking my hands so my nails dry faster, I collect myself as much as I'm able. "Thank you, then. This is more generous than anyone has a right to be. I love it here. It's just new, is all."

"Anything you need, *hija*, you just say it," Don José reminds me, and then escorts both Consuela and me to the dining room.

He's so very tall, and though he's soft around the middle, there's something about his presence that's immediately reassuring. With a small smile, it's like he's saying there's nothing in the world so harrowing that cannot be figured out. Though I feel out of place in this outfit (and if I'm being honest, in this home), Don José's sense of ease sands away the rougher edges of what's become my personality while on the road.

He escorts me as if I'm delicate, so I remember that parts of me still are.

If I can act or accept, then I choose to accept this sweet family for all of their eccentricities.

21

DINNER AND DANGER

ADELITA

Don José pulls out a chair for Consuela at the foot of the table, and then selects a seat for me halfway down the right side while we wait for Eva and the guys to join us for dinner.

"Where are the children? I haven't even seen Cordelia much since I've been back."

Consuela smiles at me. "Every now and then, they spend the night with the nanny. Otherwise, José and I would never have any time alone. Cordelia thinks she's too old for the nanny, of course, so I expect they'll be back earlier tomorrow, rather than later."

"I liked playing cars with Roberto. He's really very precious. Your children love you both; it's obvious."

I'm slipping into therapist mode, analyzing the family dynamic, which is definitely not what my role is here. I button it up after Consuela offers a sweet, "That's good to hear. They keep us on our toes, that's for sure."

Chef Aarón pours us white wine to go with our waters, and the three of us entertain small talk while we wait for Eva and the guys.

When Tio Bruno comes in, Consuela stiffens, but greets him warmly. "Good to see you, Bruno. How was your day?"

Tio Bruno tosses a dismissive hand in her direction. "The same as yesterday. The same as every day for the past week. I'm done babysitting, in case neither of you got the memo. My job is to keep Cáceres safe, not keep a perfectly healthy woman locked up all day. It's grating on my last nerve."

By the permanent tightness of his thick shoulders and the scowl that looks etched into place, I'm guessing Tio Bruno hit his last nerve many years ago.

I have nothing to add to the conversation, so I sip my water quietly. I pretend I don't see, and am not affected by, the scathing looks Tio Bruno keeps shooting in my direction.

I guess he's not thrilled about how our last conversation went down. I shouldn't be amused by that, but I can't help the ease that finds me, now that I know he's unsettled by my presence. It's clear he is used to being the one to control the temperament of any room he enters.

Mind games? Don't mind if I do.

A small smile plays on my lips.

Enjoy being at my mercy, dick.

"Is something amusing?" Tio Bruno's brusque tone cuts out of the conversation he's been having with Don José.

I refuse to let him ruin my night, though he seems intent on crushing whatever high his brother and sister-in-law are having. I set my glass of water down and tilt my head at him. "Should it be?"

Answering a question with a question is an easy way to disarm an aggressive client.

Tio Bruno doesn't know what to say to that, clearly only ever on the giving end of hostility, and not on the receiving end of limitless calm.

Type Eights on the Enneagram enjoy knowing what to expect. When they put a coin into a machine, it should always give the same results. When Tio Bruno puts aggression into the world and a tranquil smile comes back at him, the unexpected non-reaction sticks under his craw.

My sweet smile is my middle finger, and I hope he chokes on it.

Tio Bruno grumbles to himself and takes a drink of water. "Where is everyone else? I thought dinner started ten minutes ago."

And yet he showed up two minutes ago. A typical power play by a narcissist is being constantly late, making it clear that though there are external expectations, he will arrive when he deems it necessary, and everyone will be aware of his entrance.

Narcissists are exhausting.

Luckily, I have no vested interest in helping him become a better person, so I just get to play—instigating by diffusing.

Don José waves off his brother's irritation. "The dinner will keep. Ease up, Bruno. They only just got back a few hours ago. They've been on the road for over a week."

Tio Bruno fixes a cold glare on me, no doubt expecting me to squirm. Instead, I yawn.

He does not like that.

Good.

Tio Bruno's vitriol aims itself at me. "They were gone for so long because they were bringing *you* home. Plan on wasting the tribe's most valuable resources again?"

My hand goes over my heart. "Cruz, Santos and Rafi are the tribe's most precious resources? Even more than you? That's so sweet! I hope they know how much you appreciate them. Good thing you sent your top people. Wouldn't want the B Team to show up and get lost along the way. Tell me, do you lead the B Team?"

Tio Bruno's whole face puckers as if I've fed him something sour, when the thing I've fed him was a compliment for the guys under his tutelage.

Along with an insult to his ego.

The sound of shoes—not boots—shuffles down the hall. Consuela's eyes go wide. Tio Bruno's upper lip curls in disgust as if a slimy three-headed anteater has just happened upon his dining experience.

All coherent thought leaves my brain when I take in the sight of the guys in slacks and dress shirts. I've never seen them in anything other than jeans and their black t-shirts, and then pajamas. This is… a girl can only take so much.

I'm certain I'm flushed from head to toe as desire ramps up at the most inopportune time. I stand to greet them and give them a proper applause. Or, more accurately, to give Eva her proper applause, since she no doubt arranged for their attire. "Eva, what did you do?"

Eva grins like a cat with an evil vendetta, feathering her fingers. "You're right; you and I are properly dressed for dinner, and that shouldn't make us feel out of place. The boys own nice clothes, thanks to me; they just never wear them. What do you think?"

It's when I take my time to look them up and down that I realize Santos and Cruz are doing the same to me. "I think you've done a masterful job, Eva. Santos, did you…"

I didn't notice at first, not until he turns his face to the side. I'd thought his chin-length hair was pinned back. My gasp flies out and I flit to his side, running my fingers along the freshly-shaved back of his head. "You cut your hair!"

There's a boyish happiness to being doted on by me, but the tinge of insecurity shines through. "Do you like it?"

I can't stop touching it. "I love it. I mean, I love it long or short, but wow. I can see more of your face this way."

"Is that a good thing?"

I run the backs of my fingers down his cheek. "It's the best thing. You're gorgeous."

The scraping of chairs and Eva's shriek tell me I've missed something crucial in the air. The four dart to Santos, peppering him with questions.

"Did you just speak?"

"Say it again!"

"When did you get your voice back?"

"How?"

The questions keep coming, but Santos simply holds my hand, as if my approval of his haircut is the most important thing in the room. It's shaved on the sides and in the back, with the silky top just an inch and a half long. There's a small bit of gel in it, just enough to make him look stylish, like he was built for the kind of confidence that makes a man sexy. I'm used to him hiding in plain sight, ducking behind his hair and backing away from attention. Seeing his smile exposed like this?

I need to back up, or my skyrocketing libido is going to be palpable.

We never did land on a story with enough details to satisfy the family, so when Santos opens his mouth and tells them all the truth, I don't begrudge him a word of it. Honestly, I'm not sure how much they're absorbing; they're stunned he's speaking at all.

"We took Adelita to my curse tree, and she pulled out the axe. She broke my curse, so now I can speak out loud."

The explanation is succinct enough, but the questions keep on coming. Only this time, they're directed at me. They're all varying shades of the same "how" sentiment, so I respond with a shrug. "Just a lucky pull, I guess. Must've got it at the right angle."

Sure, it's a lie, but I don't expect Tio Bruno to pull his dagger from its sheath on his belt and aim it in my direction.

His upper lip is curled, but before he can utter a word, Santos steps in front of me, tucking my body behind his back. His knees are bent and his arm outstretched.

But it's Cruz who draws a gasp from me. I wouldn't have believed it if I didn't see it play out with my own two eyes. In a move so fluid, I barely understand how it happens, Cruz attacks his uncle's arm from the outside, gripping and shoving it so it wraps around Tio Bruno's body, pinning the dagger to the massive man's opposite bicep.

Then Cruz kicks at the soft spot on the underside of Tio Bruno's knees, and the towering man stumbles just enough for Cruz to lower his uncle to kneel in the center of the fray.

"Holy…" It's all I can work out before words desert me completely.

Rafael's arm coils around my waist, and he slides me backward, away from the upset. There's a steady stream of nervous cussing under his breath as goosebumps feather out over my arms. "Eva," Rafael barks over his shoulder, "let's go. Dad will sort this out."

I'm worried, sure. I've never been to a dinner where family members pulled out knives and attacked each other. But Eva is ashen, shaking at the display as she scampers to join us.

At least the kids weren't here to witness that.

"Did that just happen? Tell me that didn't happen." Eva's steps are quick enough to be a tense jog, leading us down the hallway and into… some room. Honestly, there are far too many rooms in this house to keep track of them all.

Rafael ducks us inside, standing in the doorway to listen to the argument to see which way it turns.

Eva holds onto my hand and moves us toward an antique couch that looks brand new. It's aqua, with touches of dark wood and gold trim—just like the few other furnishings in the room. At some point, I'd really like a tour of this place.

This looks like a formal sitting room, maybe to receive esteemed guests.

Eva pulls her feet up under her body, curling in a ball like a little girl. Her boldness withers as fright sets in deep. "Cruz attacked Tio Bruno. This is bad. This is very bad."

So that's how this is going to be retold.

I'm not having that.

"Actually, Tio Bruno pulled a knife on me for no good reason, and Cruz intervened. If we're talking about who needs better table manners, I'd start there."

Eva holds my hand. "Yes, I know. It's just… Tio Bruno is his commander. He's everyone's commander. Cruz just assaulted his commander." Then she stares at me, petrified and needing answers. "Cruz loves you. That's the only explanation. He would never go against Tio Bruno unless he'd clearly lost his mind."

I'm not touching that logic.

Rafael keeps his eyes trained on the hallway, but speaks to Eva. "Cruz made his choice, and I doubt he regrets it. Tio Bruno's been off his rocker for a long time, yet no one ever calls him on it. Pulling a knife on Adelita because she lifted Santos' curse? There's no way that should be allowed. He brought a fight to a celebration."

"Dad will handle it."

Rafael snorts. "You can believe that if you need to. Dad looks the other way on Tio Bruno's temper. You know that."

Eva's face pulls, as if being in the room with criticism aimed at her precious father is disgusting. I think families who are viciously protective of each other are sweet, though, studies show dynamics like that can stunt self-actualization if taken too far.

Not that anyone here cares about that sort of thing.

Incoherent shouting echoes down the halls. My stomach twists that this has all gone so poorly.

It's several minutes before I hear a door slam, and feet trotting toward us.

Santos with short hair is still shocking, and for a second, I can't focus on what he's saying. After a few blinks, his words sink in. "Tio Bruno's going to go cool down. Dad wants us to come to the table for dinner, and he doesn't want to discuss what just happened."

I can tell Santos is holding himself back, standing beside Rafi just outside the doorway. He regards me with caution, as if I have some sort of power in this situation in which I'm clearly a bystander. It looks like he doesn't know where to place his body, shifting his weight from one foot to the other uncertainly.

When I motion him to come into the room, he beelines for the spot on the couch where I'm sitting with Eva. Santos kneels, taking my free hand in his and pressing it to his cheek. "Are you alright? I was so scared he might stab you. Please don't leave us."

I did this to him—spawned this overreaction by leaving last time without warning, without a plan, and without apology. Now he's terrified that any time something goes wrong, I will take off on him again.

I comb my fingers through his hair, still familiarizing myself with the bristly shortness along the sides and back. "Nothing happened to me at all. Just some family drama I found myself in the middle of, I guess." My knuckles brush along his freshly shaved cheek. "You look so handsome. Dashing, even. All three of you. I'm sorry the moment was ruined. I feel like I did something to set it all off on the wrong path, but I can't put my finger on what it was."

"You did nothing. You're a vision, Adelita. Something out of a dream. Dad wants us to come to dinner, but if you're too upset to eat, I'll make you something else. We can go outside on the patio for dinner."

The offer is more than tempting, but I shake my head. "No. Best rip the band-aid off now, while the wound is still fresh. Otherwise things start to crust over in the wrong way, and it gets all awkward."

Santos curls my fingers into a fist and kisses my knuckles. "Not out of my sight. Not away from my side, okay?"

A small smile finds my face. "If you insist."

Santos rises and offers his hand to Eva to help her stand.

Eva wipes condensation from her lashes. "I love you in love," she rasps, her voice heady with emotion. She holds onto his hand, looking hard into his eyes. "Cruz fought Tio Bruno because he raised a knife to Adelita."

Santos nods firmly. "I know. Cruz is in love with Adelita, too."

Whoa! Dial it back.

Then Santos squeezes Eva's hand. "He and I have discussed it, and we're both happy to keep each other in the picture."

What? I mean, I knew this was the underlying subtext of what we've been dancing around, but they've talked about this?

Eva stiffens, no doubt trying to wrap her mind around all that this might mean. Though I can tell she's still digesting the information, she forces a serene expression. "Alright, then." She moves toward the door, past a speechless Rafael. "You knew about this?"

Rafael nods once. "Not my business, and definitely not yours. They've got enough knives aimed at them. They don't need lectures, too."

Her mouth snaps shut, but I can tell she's got lots to say.

So do I. "You and Cruz talked about me? He didn't say he's in love with me. He's not."

Santos kisses my cheek, and then curves his arm around my back. "I think that's a discussion for another day. I didn't make your food this time. Chef Aarón is trustworthy. But I still want to taste your food before you eat it. Is that alright?"

It's weird, but it's alright. "Sure."

Hints of me potentially being poisoned straight after having a knife pulled on me does nothing for my appetite. I was looking forward to food that didn't come from a diner or a clown's mouth, but now I feel sick to my stomach.

Even as I sit down at the table laden with far too much food, I wish I'd taken Santos up on that private patio dining experience. I can't relax, can't properly engage in conversation. In fact, for the most part, I'm practically mute. Santos speaks more than me, even when Don José asks for more details on me pulling the axe from the curse tree.

I can tell Consuela is upset, not so much about Tio Bruno, but that I'm quiet through dinner. I'm not trying to be sullen; but this whole situation has me spinning.

True to his word, Santos tries a bite off my place from every portion of my meal. Maybe it would come off as intrusive to some, but I know Santos (as much as anyone can). After living without my mom for so long and self-isolating so much, his attention to detail puts me at ease—especially considering how many times I've been snatched. I cannot imagine his stress level.

I twine my fingers through his under the table, and eat with my non-dominant hand, in hopes the connection will soothe us both. Santos is my security blanket in this foreign place where I don't understand many of the customs and rules. I want to ask about Tio Bruno, but I know that's not an option.

Why did Tio Bruno pull a knife on me? All I'd done was stand there while Santos told them I yanked his curse axe free. Wouldn't Tio Bruno want Santos' curse lifted?

A hush falls over my questions when a new thought dawns on me: if Tio Bruno really did send the Kalku after us to intercept us at the curse tree, then perhaps he didn't want Santos' curse lifted. Maybe he has an interest in keeping Santos quiet.

I nod through the rest of dinner whenever I'm required to interact, but my hold on Santos' hand turns protective.

If Tio Bruno wants Santos silent, I have to know why. I need to talk to Tio Bruno and get to the bottom of this.

I resolve myself to do all I can to make sure Santos is never silenced again.

22

TIO BRUNO'S CONTROL
ADELITA

Dinner is weighted with the memory of Tio Bruno pulling a knife on me, though we're all not speaking about it. Still, the lingering discomfort is enough to make me rush through all four courses.

The sun sets outside as we spoon dessert into our mouths, but there's been a front of gray clouds that have swooped in during the meal.

Cruz's moods are tied to the weather. As much as it makes sense to blame him for the clouds, this funk is Tio Bruno's doing. Everyone else seems to want to dismiss his bad behavior, but as it was me who had a knife pulled on her over dinner, I'm not about to let this one go. I feel no need to question the family; after this meal is over, I'm going straight to the source so we can have it out.

Don José seems to be thinking the same thing I am. "Looks like it might rain tonight. You might want to take a walk after this, kids. Some fresh air might do you some good."

I finish my dessert in four huge bites. "I think a walk

sounds nice. Good suggestion. I haven't had a chance to explore the village on my own yet."

Apparently, I've said the wrong thing. Santos and Cruz both stand, though they are not finished with their desserts. "We'll go with you," Santos explains.

"You really don't need to. You're not even finished."

As if to make a point, Santos wolfs down the rest of his dessert while standing. "There. Now I can go."

Cruz makes no show of playing along. "I know what you're doing, and no. I'm going with you, and that's that."

Eva tilts her head up at me. "What did I miss? You're not running out on us again, are you?"

My heart tugs at the glimmer of insecurity in her eyes. "Not at all. Just getting some fresh air. Don José made a good suggestion of taking a walk."

Cruz's perma-frown is in full force. "What a coincidence. That's just what I was going to do."

My shoulders lower in exasperation. "You don't need to follow me wherever I go. I'm not leaving Cáceres."

"I know exactly what you're going to do, which is why I'm going, too."

He can't possibly know I'm going to confront Tio Bruno.

Though when Cruz adds, "You're not invincible," I wonder if perhaps he does.

Rafael makes no effort to involve himself, even when I cast him a look that begs him to get a hold on the guys. He dabs at his mouth with his cloth napkin. "You brought this on yourself. Your two shadows aren't going to let you do anything reckless." He leans back in his chair. "Cruz, Santos, you should let her go, thinking she's all sneaky. Then when she tracks down Tio Bruno to confront him, you can keep an eye on her in the shadows, and jump in when she bites off more than she can chew. That way everyone wins. She gets her autonomy, and you two get to save the day."

Don José and Consuela gasp that this is my true intention. Consuela leans forward. "Troubling Tio Bruno when he's already vexed is not wise, *hija*. Best let his temper simmer."

I don't want to go against the woman who has been so kind to me, but I cannot let this rest. "He pulled a knife on me because I helped give Santos back his voice. I need to know why. If he's coming for Santos because he's upset Santos isn't silenced anymore, I won't look the other way on that. Santos deserves protection. He deserves to be heard."

Eva shakes her head. "I don't think that's why he pulled a knife on you, Adelita." Then, as if she didn't mean to speak her assumption aloud, her mouth slams shut and her neck shrinks.

My new sister has my full attention. "I would love to know why, then. I respect your need to protect him from owning up to his actions, but I feel no such compulsion to shield him like that."

Don José lowers his head. "Sit down, *hija*. Have some more water. Santos speaking has no impact on my brother. It's his latest charge that's got him on edge. The Mendez village brought in a rescue from Máximo's island. She is Máximo's daughter."

"My half-sister," I supply.

Don José straightens. "Yes. Good that Cruz told you. She looks much like you, and is just as private. No matter what Bruno tries, she will not speak a word about her time on the island. She won't even tell us her name. Bruno was reacting to that, no doubt—taking aim at a secret that's slipped by under his nose. When Santos said you pulled out the curse axe, Bruno assumed you were... I don't know, hiding something, so he drew his weapon."

I let out a forced, awkward laugh. "Hiding something? That's funny."

Rafael rolls his eyes at my act, letting me know I'm a bad liar.

I step back from the table. "My half-sister is probably scared. I'd like to meet her." I mean, honestly, who would open up to Tio Bruno?

I wonder if she's strong, like me.

Don José looks tired, his usually cheery countenance drawn downward. "As you wish it. Go on, boys. Make sure to keep an eye on her. Your uncle is in a mood."

Santos' arm touches on the small of my back, and I ignore the stern look Cruz fixes on me. The moment we step out into the gloomy twilight, I stop walking and turn toward Cruz, ignoring his severe expression. My arms snake around his shoulder, which means I have to stand on my toes.

I'm not used to hugging Cruz. He holds me in the night, sure, but this is different.

I want to get better at this, and I can tell by the way he doesn't step back from my mild affection that he is committed to the learning curve, however steep.

His body stiffens, but then he relaxes with a small chuckle as his palm finds my hip. His thumb draws a slow circle there. It's intimate, but not overtly sexual. It's a reminder that we have each other, which is nothing to sneeze at.

"I'm sorry," I offer. "The thing with your uncle? I didn't mean for everything to get so out of hand."

"Well, I hold you one-hundred percent responsible. You told him to attack you, after all." His teasing relaxes my shoulders. "One day, you'll stop apologizing for things that aren't your fault. You're my charge, and Tio Bruno knows it. I had every right to protect you from him. I wouldn't be his lead soldier if I didn't."

"Still, I'm sorry." My arms slip down until my hands rest on his chest. He's so very broad and muscular, yet in moments like these, he's an utter softy.

"I'm a big boy, Addy." There's a low rumble, almost a purr in his chest that vibrates under my touch. I love the feel of it, so I spread my palms over his pectorals, rubbing lightly in slow circles.

Am I groping him?

I am.

I should stop.

When his eyes go wide, I realize how much I'm carrying on, so I jerk backward, tucking my hands behind my back. "Sorry." My cheeks are hot now.

I blame the dress. It's making me more daring than I should be with someone who is so very calloused.

I turn toward the fading sunlight. "Which way to Tio Bruno's dungeon?"

Santos chuckles. "The barracks are this way." He motions for me to take the lead, but as I've only been there once, I slink back to Santos' side. My hand falls in his, but it only rests there a second before he pulls away. "You can't hold my hand in public, *mi amor*."

The quick jolt of shame washes through me. "What? You don't want to hold my hand?"

Santos scrabbles to explain. "Of course I do, but in Cáceres, I'm the savage. They will be scared for your safety if you're seen on my arm. I'll walk behind, like I do with the guys. It will make the villagers feel safer."

Anger flares up, boiling under my epidermis. "You're not a savage! And I don't have a precious reputation that's more important than you. You're my equal, or we're nothing."

Santos rubs the nape of his neck. "It's not that simple."

"It's exactly that simple. They are afraid of you because you're always hiding who you are. They can't appreciate anything new because it's not as safe for them as looking in a mirror. You're a wonderful man, Santos. No need to lurk in the shadows. Best let them see you as you are."

Santos and Cruz exchange looks of uncertainty. This is way too complicated for a simple walk.

I whirl on Cruz because he's the nearest native. My finger points in his face as I gear up for a lecture. "This is what's wrong with the walls surrounding Cáceres. They tell enemies they're not welcome here, sure, but they also communicate that anything off center of the way things have always been is something to fear, something the people need protection against. You are a superior fighter because of Santos marrying your style with his. You evolved because you saw past your people's prejudice. But mark my words, as long as those walls are standing, no one in Cáceres will grow stronger. They have cut off their growth, so this city, these ideas and this people will only manage to make themselves smaller. It's disgusting." I step back, standing beside Santos. "And it's communicated to your brother that he's less than."

Cruz holds up his hands in surrender. "You're welcome to tell everyone exactly that. It's not my wall, Addy. I didn't build it."

"But you aren't standing up for your brother when it cuts his confidence in half. Silence is agreement. He looks to you for acceptance, and you're accepting this wall. I will not accept that he doesn't deserve things like a girlfriend just because he was born outside of this village, and neither should you."

Santos touches my arm. "It's okay. Really. It's not Cruz's fault."

"I will not stand for you to be halfway liberated. You were promised a new start here, but their prejudice won't give it to you." I shake my head, extending my hand to his. "I won't let them question your right to be a person and take up space here. Not on my watch."

Finally, Santos' hand slips into mine, and we start on our path. Cruz walks behind us, acting as our sentry. I thought this was a safe village, the harbor from the harshness, but Cruz and Santos are still on their guard. I wonder how much of that is just who they are, no matter the surroundings.

A few people stop what they are doing to stare at us. One woman lets loose a muffled scream, as if she's trying to warn me I'm an idiot to be near someone so dangerous.

It's not unlike my first walk to the barracks, where I was at Cruz's side, and endured the villagers murmuring and giving me looks of horror, as if I was walking next to a monster who might murder me.

I mean, they weren't entirely wrong on the monster part. Though, Cruz and I seem to be getting along much better as of late.

As I walk through the chilled night under the dimming, cloudy sun, the villagers react similarly. They are staring in shock, as if they can't believe Santos can walk on two legs, let alone wear a dress shirt and fitted trousers. Some drop their bundles on the ground and gape at the sight of Santos with a woman.

Or maybe they're horrified that I've dared don a fancy white dress, undeserving of this luxury as I am. I cling tighter to Santos' hand, which I realize is sweating.

I'm making him nervous.

I've forced him to stand up for himself, rather than focusing my vitriol on the people who are oppressing him and calling it citizenship.

I drop Santos' grip and let my steps fall a few behind his. His gait is jerky now, and his backside tight (not that I'm staring) as we walk the rest of the way to the barracks.

I'm never going to fit in here.

Santos leads the way through many cavernous concrete halls, our steps echoing and announcing us as intruders. Though Santos and Cruz don't seem all that shaken to be here, I'm aware that I am out of my element. I wanted to question Tio Bruno about why he pulled a knife on me, but with every step I take, it's clear that I don't have any position of power in here.

I might meet my sister.

It still hasn't fully hit me that I have a blood relative. I never had an aunt or uncle, never had a cousin. My dad didn't want me, and my mom, saint though she is, passed away before I stopped needing her to be all of those things for me.

And now I have a sister. A sister whom my father kept. He didn't want me. He wanted her.

How old is she? Does she also enjoy helping people? Is she a good cook? Maybe she can teach me one of our father's recipes. Is she freakishly strong, too?

When we reach a door with too many locks on it, I know we've reached Tio Bruno's personal chambers. I assumed he had his own place outside the barracks, but when he answers Cruz's knock and ushers us inside, I can see by the sofa sleeper pulled out in the corner that he resides here.

I do not like, nor do I trust this man, but sadness sweeps over my features when I realize this is how consumed with work Tio Bruno's life has become.

I suppose I would be surly if I lived in this concrete bunker, too.

"What do you want?" Tio Bruno asks Cruz, ignoring Santos and me.

Cruz doesn't beat around the bush. "Adelita wants to meet her half-sister. She also wants to know why you pulled a knife on her for lifting Santos' curse. She thinks you must want Santos mute because of your reaction."

Santos says nothing.

As much as I want to shrink into the background, I lift my chin. It's not an insane theory. Though, as my logic catches Tio Bruno by surprise, I'm guessing I'm not quite right.

Tio Bruno's scowl recovers. "I don't have to explain myself to you. My job is to protect the tribe." His focus shifts to me, and I'm reminded of how huge and formidable the man before me is. "If I felt you were a danger to Cáceres, it's my duty to follow that hunch to its answer. I can live with being wrong. Though, I'm not entirely certain I am. You pulled a curse axe out of the tree? You realize Cruz, Rafael and I have all tried, and it stayed stuck."

I draw myself up as much as I can. "You big, strong men must've loosened it for me," I simper, batting my lashes because if he's allowed to be a brat, so am I.

Tio Bruno moves closer, though not quick enough to be deemed a threat. Santos stiffens, but doesn't intervene as Tio Bruno uses his height and bulk to tower over me, looking me dead in the eye. "What a sweet little lie that was. The only question is why."

"Why would I lie to you?" My heart is hammering, so I remind myself that I am stronger than this military man. All he has are words, and I have buckets of those.

"That's the big question, isn't it. You didn't pull out the axe. One of the guys finally figured out how." His guess is completely wrong, but I have no desire to correct him on it.

"Interesting thing," I say, tilting my head to the side. "When we got there, the Kalku were waiting. Funny, that. You were the only one who knew we were headed there."

This catches him by surprise.

Cruz hisses. "I told her you didn't leak our location to anyone. You wouldn't send the Kalku to hurt us."

I've just about had it with this family protecting the biggest baby of all. "Oh, really?" Arms akimbo, my attitude flies free. "We tell him that's where we're headed, and he sends the Kalku after us. Then when he sees they failed in blocking us from getting Santos' curse axe out of the tree, he pulls a knife on me."

Tio Bruno looks startled that the logic makes so much sense. "That's what you think?"

"Prove me wrong."

Tio Bruno takes a step back, holding up his hands to diffuse the glare aimed at him. "There was one other person in the room when you all told me you'd be heading to the curse tree. You went there against orders, might I add," he tags on, narrowing his eyes at Cruz. "I'll not punish you for defending your charge at dinner tonight, but going against my orders to come home? I don't care how your little witch over here stilted the conversation to get you out of coming back, you let it happen, Cruz."

"So did you," I argue. Though, when Cruz holds up his hand to silence me, I can tell I've said the wrong thing.

Cruz is steady while Tio Bruno and I are controlled by our heated tempers. "That's fair. Show Adelita her sister first. Santos can stay with her. I'll stay right here until you and I are past it."

"That might take a while."

Their exchange makes me think Cruz is taking the blame for me worming us out of the order to come home, instead of going to the curse tree. I don't know what it all means, but no part of this sounds functional—in military terms, or in familial relations.

There's a gravity to Cruz's nod, telling us to go on without him.

"I don't like this," I protest, not understanding all the nuances, but gleaning enough to be able to form my own opinion. "I'm not leaving you with him when he's clearly in a mood."

Cruz's upper lip curls at me. The look is so vitriolic that I recoil. "I told you to go with Santos, Adelita. I'm not sure what was confusing about that. When I say move, you move. You're not cut out for this." When I hesitate, he shouts. "Go!"

His words whip across my chest, causing me to flinch. "Why are you being like this?"

But I know why. He's in front of Tio Bruno. The level at which I matter to him has now shifted, moving me to the bottom rung of importance. Tears prick my eyes as my shoulders go concave.

I cower into Santos' side, but I don't bother speaking up again. Tio Bruno gives Santos a key and directs him which room to go to.

From the safe distance of the doorway, I speak once more to Tio Bruno. "What is her name? My sister," I ask, making it clear that I won't run just because Cruz raises his voice like a child.

"I don't know," Tio Bruno admits, and I can tell he's ashamed at this lack of knowledge. Vulnerability pokes through his armor, which is a curious thing to witness. "She hasn't spoken a word. Won't let our healer treat her, either."

"Is she injured?"

"She was limping when they brought her in."

Santos leads me out of Tio Bruno's office/bedroom before I can get more information, but dread bubbles in my stomach.

"It's better this way," Santos whispers. "Tio Bruno needs to know Cruz is still under his command. Cruz needs to show his uncle that he's still a good soldier."

"Under his control. This is sick."

Santos shrugs, like he can't bother to contemplate the difference.

I don't like the idea of leaving Cruz with a man who has a very clear "I'm going to punish you" vibe about him.

But I put one foot in front of the other, hoping my new family will be nothing like Cruz's.

23

IDENTICAL

SANTOS

Adelita is upset. I can't stand when she's uneasy. But this is nothing we didn't expect. Ignoring Tio Bruno's orders to come straight home has consequences. Cruz knew what he was doing when he didn't turn the car around. He'll get drilled through a grueling row of calisthenics, plus whatever else Tio Bruno needs to do to ensure his place at the top.

It's sweet that none of this dawned on her. She was so surprised, scandalized that there is punishment for disobedience in the military.

Cruz shouted at Adelita to get her out of there. He doesn't like her near Tio Bruno.

I can't say I blame him.

Still, I don't like the way she trembles beside me. If I'm guessing right, she didn't have a life surrounded by anger and yelling. This is all a culture shock for her, so we walk slowly. My arm curls around her as we fall in step with each other. The villagers don't come into the barracks, and the soldiers only work during the day, unless there's some sort of emergency, so the halls are empty for the most part.

Adelita is a ball of nerves from head to toe, wrapped in a white gown that begs me to appreciate just how much of a woman she is. I wish I could take her back to her bedroom and relax her, but if I had a chance to see Santiago, I wouldn't be able to rest simply because I needed to.

If Santiago wasn't dead, I would be able to introduce my twin brother to the fine woman who lets me hold onto her. He would be shocked, seeing me dressed in slacks with my hair cut. I'm still getting used to that.

Santiago wouldn't think I was a savage. He'd tell me I was a king.

The key slides into the lock when we reach the chamber Tio Bruno indicated. I wish we weren't here, but the fact that this woman is locked in what's basically an upgraded cell means this woman is dangerous, or at the very least, untrusted.

I step back when I pop the door open, letting Adelita get first look. She opens her mouth, but no words come out.

She's never had a sibling before, and I can tell she's freezing up, unsure how to make contact. She's got that frightened look about her—fight or flight—so I move into the room, absorbing the shock alongside her.

"How did…" I begin, but then stop myself. It was easier when no one expected me to speak. I didn't have to force sense into a confusing situation. When I take in the woman who could be Adelita's twin, all intelligent speech deserts me.

Adelita's silence tells me she is stuck in the same conundrum.

The room hasn't changed since I was rescued from the Kalku and stored here for safe keeping. It wasn't until Tio Bruno deemed me as not being a threat that I was allowed to move about freely. The concrete box offers no warmth. The cot in the corner has a thin mattress that gives way to the support bars beneath. There's a steel toilet and sink in the corner, and a table with a chair.

The chair is to sit in while Tio Bruno interrogates you. He likes to be taller, intimidating and in control. I don't begrudge him any of those things, but it's unsettling all the same.

The woman stands, and I can see she's favoring her right leg. I wonder how long her injury has gone unchecked.

Adelita and her sister gape at each other. Though Adelita knew her sister would be here, no one expected them to look so very similar.

The woman clearly was never told that her sister was coming. She's stunned into silence, though I wonder, from the information Tio Bruno gave, if she is mute.

I want to leave the two of them alone so they can have their moment, but no part of me is willing to leave Adelita with someone I haven't vetted.

"Hello," I begin lamely.

Rafi would know what to say. He has a thousand words that can put people at ease. I show up, and everyone tenses.

It's then I realize her shock has shifted from Adelita to me, as if my presence is the scandal. "What are you doing here?" she asks me, her voice barely above a whisper. "Did he let you go?"

So she can talk. She just didn't want to give her words to Tio Bruno.

Can't argue with her judgment.

I don't know who "he" is. Tio Bruno, maybe? Instead of asking her, I tilt my head to the side. I'm better at nonverbal communication than figuring out the right words to say.

"Has the sun set?" She looks crazed with anxiety as she shouts. "Has the sun set?"

I nod slowly. "Only just."

A cry of relief comes from her lips. "Father would never

let you come for me. Did you…" She pauses, limping toward me. "Did you escape? We both escaped?" Then a cry so desperate yanks from her lips that my heart jerks in my chest. She falls forward into my arms, which scramble to hold her upright as she begins sobbing. "I thought when they rescued me that I would never see you again! I fought them at first. I told them I couldn't leave the island without you!"

I can't put the pieces together because nothing makes a lick of sense. But I don't tell her that. I simply offer my support, figuring that's what I should do for my girlfriend's sister when she's out of sorts.

It's when her lips touch my cheek that my words find me in the form of a protest. "No! I don't know who you think I am, but I don't know you! You can't kiss me!"

I can't get her off me fast enough. Even though she shrieks in pain at my words, as if they're purposefully cruel, I hold to them. I'm shocked with horror, and immediately fall to my knees. I only want Adelita's lips to touch my skin. But her sister kissed my cheek so near my lips that I'm tailspinning with terror.

My skin burns as I press my forehead to the floor, lacing my fingers at the base of my nape. "I didn't know she would do that! I'm sorry, Adelita. I'm sorry!"

Adelita is the only calm voice in the room, though I can tell she's fighting for serenity by the quaver in her tone. "Do you know who this is?" she asks her sister calmly as she descends to her knees before me.

No, no. I pop up, forsaking a proper debasement for the sake of undoing one very important wrong. "You don't kneel. No, my heart. You stand. I'm to kneel. I wronged you."

Adelita's fingers tangle in my hair as we both rise. "You didn't do anything wrong. Are you okay? I can tell you didn't want that to happen."

"You're the only woman who kisses me! I would never... I'm sorry!"

Adelita presses her finger to my lips without a hint of condemnation as she turns to her sister. "Why did you kiss him?" she asks, not in accusation, but as a genuine question. "You don't know him."

Adelita's sister is utterly distraught. "Santiago, why are you acting like this? You're my only friend in this whole mess! Don't pretend you don't know me. I should have stayed and made sure not to leave the island without you, but it all happened so fast! I told them to turn back for you, but they wouldn't listen!"

Every cell in my body feels like it's frozen on impact at hearing her words. "Santiago? You think I'm Santiago?"

Tears bloom and roll down her cheeks. "Don't pretend like this! If I could have made the rescue team to take me back so we could find you, I would have! They wouldn't listen. Please don't do this!" The woman takes in Adelita with palpable heartbreak painted across her face. "I wronged your boyfriend, and now he's pretending he doesn't know me."

Adelita is so graceful that she recovers easily, remaining calm when I'm verging on the edge of hysterical. "And you think this is Santiago?"

The woman nods emphatically. "He's my friend."

"I see. And how long ago did you last see him?"

"I met him when Father had me abducted and taken to his island. Santiago was supposed to watch over me and keep his distance, but we look after each other. Most days, Santiago was all I had. The last time I saw him was the day before I was rescued from the island. I don't know how many days or weeks it's been." Then she turns to me, her tears of heartbreak mutating to betrayal. "Tell her!"

But I have no words. It's not possible. My brother died two years ago.

"Stay right here," Adelita instructs. She holds up her hands, making sure not to touch me as she addresses her sister. "I will help you figure this out. Santiago I'm sure would never pretend not to know you. Tell me your name. I've always wanted a sister, but this is starting out dreadfully."

"Tavita." Agony still wells in the woman's features. "You look just like your picture. You're four years younger than me."

Adelita braces herself on the doorframe, forcing a watery smile to hold. "My picture? You knew about me?"

Tavita nods slowly. "Not before Father had me taken to the island, but yeah. I know about you."

Adelita meets her sister's gaze and nods. "I'm glad to meet you, Tavita. I'm sorry we upset you. But please believe us when I tell you that this man is not Santiago. This is Santiago's identical twin, Santos."

Wonder pushes out the betrayal on Tavita's face. "Santos?"

It's too much. I can't make sense of this mess. This was supposed to be Adelita's big moment, but now it's...

She's wrong. That's all there is to it. I saw my brother murdered in front of my own two eyes.

I scramble away and bolt down the hall, knowing there is one person who will always tell me how the world works when I'm too new to its twists and turns.

I need my brother.

I need Cruz.

24

SISTERS AND STORIES
CRUZ

I'm sweating as I grit my teeth through too many pushups. Tio Bruno's boot is heavy on my shoulder, but I don't let him know the resistance hurts my joints. I don't bother asking how many I'm to do; I keep muscling through the exhaustion and pain, knowing my uncle is making me a better soldier. I'll be stronger after this, more useful to the tribe. I took off my shirt and undershirt before we began, which is just as well. Condensation mattes my chest and arms, and a drip of sweat trickles down my face, tickling my nose.

It's not until Santos bolts into the room that I pause.

He's signing to me, though it's not to keep his words from Tio Bruno, who speaks enough sign to get by. Santos is signing his brother's name over and over, which makes me wonder if he's having some sort of mental fit.

"I didn't tell you to stop," Tio Bruno chides me in his cold tone.

"What's wrong, Santos?" I ask as I pick back up in my steady rhythm. Up, down. Up, down. I lost count a long time ago, but I know it's more than three hundred.

Santos is still signing, but I can't get a good look at his fingers from this angle.

"You have to speak out loud, Brother. I can't see all that well from down here."

A broken cry belts out. "Santiago! She says Santiago is alive!"

It's the only thing that brings my body to a stop. "What?"

"Keep going," Tio Bruno commands.

But I don't bother to listen. This is more important. My punishment can wait. "What happened, Santos?"

He's gaunt and looks positively terrified. "Tavita. That's Adelita's sister. She thought I was Santiago! She said he was on the island with her, watching her for Máximo. She says she saw him as recently as the day before she was rescued by the Mendez soldiers! That was only last month, right? She can't have seen him, Cruz! My brother is dead!"

When I pull myself to my feet without permission, I know it's both the right thing to do, and also the wrong thing. "Get back down here," Tio Bruno tells me, his face stern. "I'm not finished with you, boy."

"Yeah? Well, I'm finished with you, old man." My teeth grind whenever he disrespects me by calling me a boy. "Me setting things square between us isn't as important as Santos' brother possibly being alive. Shame on you for looking out for your pride instead of looking out for your people."

I know it's going to cost me, but I don't care. Santos is my brother, and he needs me. I leave my discarded button-up and undershirt behind, dashing out the door and following Santos' lead. I wipe the sweat off my face as I run, trying to piece together anything that forces this to make sense.

Santiago is dead. We all saw him die. I tried to liberate them both, but he was stabbed by the jackal they call Father. The rule is to kill off the slaves if they're in danger of being taken. Better to have them dead than bastardized by the outside world.

We round the corner and dart into the cell Santos used to stay in when we first brought him here. That he has the strength to go inside now tells me how much he loves Adelita and needs to be near her during his moment of upset.

Adelita is positively ashen, riddled with shock, though not without her wits about her. "Cruz," she greets me. "Th-this is my s-sister, Tavita."

She steps back from me, wary I'll blast her with the temper I let flare just minutes ago. I don't like the sight of Adelita shoving her body into the corner, controlled panic painting her features.

I forgot how devastatingly gorgeous Adelita is tonight. All nights, really, but tonight in particular. She's a beauty wrapped in a white dress. Everything about her reminds me how wrong I was to keep her cooped up in the car, eat out of drive-through windows, and survive on anything less than the best.

She's the finest woman I've ever seen, and I'm a sweaty, shirtless slob.

A sweaty slob who yelled at her to go away. I didn't want Tio Bruno to turn his anger onto her. He can do what he likes to me, but Adelita? I didn't want to hurt her feelings, but if that's what it takes to protect her from him when he's in a mood, I guess that's what's going to happen.

When my gaze falls on Tavita, I can't hold back my surprise. "You look so much alike." Tavita appears to be a few years older, and maybe a couple inches taller, but everything else is strikingly similar. Heart-shaped face, long inky eyelashes, disarmingly blue eyes and a warmth to their umber skin.

I shake off the shock and get down to business, confirming with Tavita that yes, Santiago is very much alive on the island with Máximo, enslaved and working as a sentry of sorts.

Tavita sits on her cot, shoulders slumped as tears roll down her cheeks. "I thought you were Santiago," she tells Santos. "I can't leave him there. He's being used by my dad. Father treats him terribly, demanding far too much. Santiago is a good man. All of the slaves there are."

Santos is breathing in rough pants. "Santiago was stabbed. I saw the light go out in his eyes."

Tavita shrieks. "What? When? He can't be dead!"

I take the only seat in the room, wondering where the urge to tug Adelita to sit on my thigh comes from. I resist it. I mean, she's a grown woman, and I'm in need of a shower.

Plus, I yelled at her. No matter my reason, I don't want her to forgive me and flirt with me after I unleash like that.

I run my hand over my face, which is still damp. "What Santos means to say is that his twin brother, Santiago, was stabbed on March 1st, two years ago. We were positive he died that day. But it sounds like you've seen him since then."

Adelita looks like she might be sick.

Tavita dabs at her eyes with the sleeve of the stained white undershirt she was given to wear. "No, he didn't die two years ago. Obviously. I was trading ghost stories with him the day before I was liberated from the island. So, however long ago that was. Two weeks? A month? No idea."

Santos leans against the far wall and slides down the length of it, plopping down on the cold floor with his knees gathered to his chest. He looks like a little boy like that, afraid and unsure of the world.

I have to fix it. He's my brother. My responsibility.

I ask question after question, unsure if I'm getting a bigger picture of the whole thing, or if I'm only adding more uncertainty to the mix.

Tavita answers everything quickly and without the scent

of a lie. I have no reason to doubt her. She looks scared and confused when she fixes me with a worried stare. "Santiago knows you think he's dead. Said he was surprised he lived through it all and was sent to Máximo." Her voice lowers. "Sometimes he wishes he was dead, rather than working for Máximo. Others have tried to escape the island loads of times, but Massacooramaan killed them all."

A mournful sound comes from Santos.

Tavita is finally talking, so I keep the train going as long as possible. "What does Santiago do there?"

"Basic security," she replies. "He heals anyone who's injured. When I was kidnapped and brought to the island, he was my guard. Had to make sure I got food and water. Things like that. He's miserable. Has to do what Máximo wants, or he gets shocked." She points to her ankle. "Wears a band just there. If Máximo is upset with Santiago, he shocks him." Tavita's gaze turns foggy, like she's picturing a memory. "One of the times I tried to escape, Máximo shocked Santiago so much and so often, he was limping for a week after I was recovered. I learned that escape wasn't in the cards for me."

Santos is rocking back and forth. I want to send him away so he doesn't have to hear this, but it's his twin brother. He deserves to know the truth, however horrific it might be.

But Tavita isn't paying attention to us. She's lost in her story, in her heartbreak. Tio Bruno couldn't get a word out of her, but she's spilling everything to us. "I took care of him after that. When he brought me my food, he would stay and I'd work on his leg." Her gaze darts to me. "I'm a physical therapist. Or I was, before I was taken. Now I'm a nothing."

At this, Adelita speaks up. Though she's still plastered to the far corner, palming both walls, her voice is soothing. "Your profession is not the whole of who you are. What else do you like about yourself?"

Tavita glances up. "I hardly remember anymore. My real life was so long ago. I lived alone before I was taken." Her eyes tear up all over again. "I'm not sure anyone but my job and my landlord even noticed I'd disappeared."

The sisters are alike in more ways than just looks, it seems.

"That was this one, too," I say, jabbing my thumb in Adelita's direction. Without looking, I know Adelita is glaring at me for ratting out her hermit ways to her sister. "Similar faces, same eyes, same loner way to you both."

Adelita shrinks, if possible, even further into her corner. She likes knowing people, but she hates being known.

Tough.

"Who cares that I had no friends?" Addy shouts, and I can tell she's hit her last nerve. "My sister doesn't need that information."

I stand, taking a step toward Adelita, but I make sure to keep enough distance so she doesn't spook and run. "Look, I know you're mad at me. I didn't want Tio Bruno to come after you, so I had to get you out of there."

"There are about a dozen other ways that could have been accomplished."

"I see that now. Are we cool?"

Judging by her disgust, I'm guessing that was the wrong thing to say.

"We are not cool! None of this is cool! My sister was abducted! Did my mom know about her? I've had a sister all this time, and she was abducted? I have a sister, Cruz! How is that possible? And what about Santiago? Santiago's been alive all this time, but as a captive? My boyfriend's brother is currently my father's slave? And the timeline is off! How is no one addressing that? Nothing about this situation is cool!"

If Santos was himself, he would hug Adelita so she has a safe place to fall apart. If Rafi was here, he'd kiss her lips and hold her. He'd conjure up some lie to make her think every-thing was all going to be fine. Because it's Rafi, she would believe it.

But I'm all she has, and I'm terrible at this sort of thing.

Do I want to be terrible at this? Would Adelita push me away if I tried to comfort her? Even if I'm bad at it, would she appreciate the effort and let it soothe her?

I move slowly, offering up my arms because that seems the thing to do.

Addy is just as uncertain of the embrace as it unfolds. The smallest touch is electric. Maybe it's because my sweat has dried from the unyielding chill in the barracks, leaving me freezing and shirtless. Maybe it's because women usually give me a wide berth, so any contact is earthshattering.

Beyond both of those reasons, I am certain goosebumps are breaking out all over my arms simply because it's Adelita.

Her trust is addictive, so I swim in the sensation like a glutton when her head finally rests against my bare chest. She's stiff at first, so I wonder if I'm doing it wrong, but then she releases her tension in a gust that fans across my nipple, tightening everything inside of me as she relaxes in my arms. "I'm scared, Cruz. I don't know what it all means."

My hand moves up and down her spine. "I know, baby. You don't like surprises."

I cringe that I called her a cutesy nickname. I sound like an idiot. She should push me away.

Instead, she snorts, which I find endearing. "I really don't. None of it makes sense."

I can feel the heat from her bosom as it warms my chest. This dress draws my eye like nothing else. I'm a lovestruck teenager every time I look at her in it. "Then hold onto me. Just take a few breaths. It's not a race to figure it all out."

Except if Santiago really is alive and in captivity, I know

where we will be going next. Whether Tio Bruno sends us or not, I'll be leading the guys straight to the island.

I hold tighter to Addy, knowing she's not going to take well to our separation. But we can't bring her to Máximo. That's just what he'd want.

I can't let him anywhere near the woman in my arms. She trusts me.

Even when she shouldn't.

25

VANILLA DREAMS

CRUZ

*I*t's difficult to get Santos and Addy back to the house, but after I promise she can see her sister in the morning, Adelita finally lets me lead her away. And where Addy goes, Santos is sure to follow.

He's shaking as he walks behind us, using the brightness of Addy's dress to guide his unstable steps. He needs fruit or something to perk up his mind.

Really, what he needs is sleep, though I can't imagine he'll get a wink after learning his twin brother is still alive.

The sun has long since set, so no one is out to give me a hard time for having Adelita tucked under my arm while we walk in step with each other. It's like once I got her in my arms, she realized she wasn't ready to be anywhere else.

Good. I like her right here.

Eva races to the backdoor the second we cross over the threshold. Seeing our grave expressions, she skids to a halt. "What happened?"

I shake my head. "Adelita met her sister. Santiago is still alive."

"What?!" Eva screeches.

I hold up my free hand to quell her volume. "We can talk about it all in the morning. The two of them are battling some serious shock. Can you help me get them into bed?"

Eva is brimming with questions, I can tell, but she stuffs them down and nods emphatically. "Pajamas," she suggests. "I'll have Aarón make some steamed milk with vanilla beans. He's in bed now, so it might take a few, but I'll wake him. I can help Adelita if you can help Santos."

"Deal." I make to hand Adelita off to my sister, but the little beauty clings to me, as if she can't bear to be parted from my side. "Baby," I coo, not caring that my sister is hearing me be sweet to Addy. I can't stop myself. I was mean to her on purpose tonight. I will never do that again. "It's alright."

"No. It's not alright. Act or accept. Act or accept." She's muttering to herself. I doubt she knows she's speaking aloud. "'Evil only needs permission to thrive.' This all happened because good people stayed silent."

"Baby." I need to stop calling her that. "It can't be solved tonight."

Addy looks up at me with worry lining her eyes. "Can we sleep with you tonight?"

My heart swells and my whole body warms. She's not asking because she's worried about La Sayona, pitying my plight. She wants to be near me because she wants to be comforted. She wants to feel safe.

I give her that.

My chest puffs without me telling it to. "Every night," I promise. "Take off this dress and come to my bedroom."

My eyes widen at the blatant invitation. Luckily, only Eva is coherent enough to catch how sleazy I sound. My sister balks at me, but thankfully, doesn't comment on it. I surrender Addy to her care, but instantly wish it was me helping her into her pajamas.

I turn to Santos, who is unresponsive. Even after I hug him and kiss his cheek, he's still not himself. Santos stares vacantly ahead, following me to his bedroom only when I give a light tug on his arm, directing his steps.

I don't relish picking out clean pajamas for another dude, but Santos is my brother, and he needs me to look after him while the shock settles. I have to resort to ordering him to change, since nothing else is getting through. He doesn't respond to my quiet request, only registering harsh authority. "After you change and brush your teeth, you'll come to my room, alright? I'll watch over you. Santos, say it back to me."

"Change. Teeth. Your room."

I give him some space to change and meander into my bedroom, welcoming the shower and the ability it has to mute out all other sounds. Though, if either of them needs me, I won't be able to hear them. My relaxing shower quickly becomes a race as I lather up and rinse off in record time.

When I step out and towel off, there's no sign that they were in distress without me. Rafi, Santos and Adelita are mine to look after. That much, I've known for a long time. But this tug I feel for them? It's a magnet attached to a panic button that goes off inside of me if there's a hint of them being unhappy.

This is stressful.

I search for my flannel pajama pants, which I finally find stuffed in the wrong drawer.

Rafi.

He's always moving my stuff to drive me insane.

I pull on the soft pajama pants, not bothering with a shirt when I hear a rustle coming from my bedroom.

The new bed Eva had brought in is a feat of engineering, indeed. It's larger than my usual king-size.

When I see Addy standing near the foot of the bed, she

looks tiny compared to the massive thing. She's utterly lost, holding herself around the middle. She's wearing a pink robe that falls a few inches above her naked knees. At first, I wonder if she's anxious about the bed, taking in the grand scope of the thing. But when she turns her chin to me, I can see that she's too overwhelmed by the evening to make sense of anything. Her hair is up in a curly bun, with tendrils dangling down to tease her neck.

To tease me.

I want to kiss her so badly.

But not tonight. She's not herself. Not in a good headspace. Also, I yelled at her.

My hands are gentle and my movements slow as I help her into the bed, pulling down the covers that have been sprayed with a lavender scent. I'll bet that's Consuela's doing. She's been eyeing Addy ever since we got back, pushing us together. It wasn't lost on me that the dress Consuela picked out for Addy to wear tonight was nothing short of a wedding gown.

Not that I didn't enjoy it, but still. Real subtle.

Addy slips out of her bathrobe with no hint of cunning as she crawls to the middle of the mattress. The nightgown is so short that I'm treated to a glimpse of her lace-covered backside. She's wearing a low-cut, very short strappy little number that makes me feel instantly overdressed. She doesn't bat her lashes at me or give me a sexy kitten look, even though she's dressed for the part. She merely lays on her side in the bed with her hands tucked under her cheek, like she's never had an indecent thought in her life.

I love her curvy hips. Like, want to bite them, pinch them.

I climb into the bed beside her, loving the way she migrates to my body. She cuddles near to me as I sit up with my back against the solid wood of the headboard.

My arms fall around her, cradling her while I take a

chance and kiss the top of her head.

Easy, boy.

My hand trills slowly up and down her arm, just the way I know she likes it. How badly I want to slide her strap off her shoulder, taking the rest of this slip of fabric with it. Her nipples are taut, standing at attention through the veil of pink silk.

As much as I love the sight, I know erect nipples means she's chilly, so I fold the comforter over our laps like the smitten man I am.

"You want to talk about it?"

Who am I, asking something like that? I sound like my sister, or like Dad.

She shakes her head. "Just don't leave. Stay right here."

That, I can do. I'm not sure a five-alarm emergency could pry me from her. She's so trusting as she rests against me, her cheek on my chest, her forehead in the crook of my neck. She lets me stroke her arm, relaxing her while I excite myself for no good reason.

Instead of admitting all that, I reply with a simple, "Whatever you like."

"Whatever I like?" she echoes, twisting my words with a question mark. She pulls her head back so she can stare up at me, her eyes blinking with something I cannot decipher.

"I'm yours for the night." Why did my voice drop half an octave?

She's not put out by my poor choice of words. Instead, she reaches up and strokes my jaw, feeling the sharp edge as she traces from just below my ear down to my chin, and then back again. Her touch is painfully slow, seducing me almost as much as the sight of her lace panties.

Her thumb traces the dip of my lower lip, and without her saying a word, my lips part, because I'm pretty sure that's what she wants. "Addy, I..."

…I want to strip off your clothes before I've even properly kissed you?

…I invited you into my bed and can't stop thinking about your nipples on a day your life took a disturbing turn?

…You're in love with my brother and best friend, but I'm also in…

I cannot finish my sentence. Instead, I let her thumb guide me as it tilts my chin lower, angling my face so I can more easily slant my lips to hers.

When a knock nags my attention from the reason my heart is pounding, I cuss so loud, it makes her jump in my arms. "Sorry. Come on in." It's probably Santos, finally ready to turn in.

Instead, it's Aarón, who bustles in with a tray, holding three mugs. Instinctually, I tug the comforter up over Addy's shoulder, hiding her body from view. Aarón doesn't need to know how pert her nipples still are.

"Eva requested steamed milk for you, Miss Adelita and Santos. Has Santos perhaps lost his way? He's wandering the halls. Shall I fetch him for you?"

"Thanks, Aarón. Santos is a little out of sorts, so don't spook him. Bring him on in here."

"Very good, Cruz."

I'm kicking myself for not kissing her when we had our moment alone. Though I'm certain Santos is fine with me making a move (so long as I don't steal Adelita away from him), I don't want to kiss her for the first time with an audience.

I want to take my time with her.

Preferably not on a day she's so out of it, she can barely put one foot in front of the other.

I hand Adelita her mug, molding her fingers around it. She resituates but doesn't want to lose the contact between us. My girl leans her back against the left half of my torso, letting me prop her up while we both sip our steamed milk. With my free hand, I brush my knuckles down the silk of her cheek, stroking the side of her throat while she swallows a few demure gulps.

I could do this for hours—pet her and spend my time guessing if my fingers are fondling bare skin or silk.

I cannot stop touching her, not even when Aarón escorts Santos into the room and helps him into bed on her other side.

Santos' vacant expression is the only thing that stills my movements. I grab up the third mug and press it into his grip, using my authoritative tone to command him to drink it.

He obeys without blinking, still mired in shock.

Adelita removes herself from my chest and snuggles into Santos, kissing his cheek. It's the only thing that brings him marginally back to himself. He takes another drink and then kisses her lips, just once. "Santiago," he whispers to her, communicating his agony in a single word.

"I know. We will find him."

I don't bother correcting her. It's too late at night for a fight about it. But there's no way she's going anywhere near Máximo.

Santos drains his mug far quicker than either of us, and then kisses her again. He lays his head on his pillow, and miracle of miracles, his eyes drift closed. I thought for sure he'd be restless and pacing all night.

Sleepiness overtakes me in the next few breaths, but I fight it until Adelita finishes her drink and hands me her mug. I set them on the end table, noting how right they look together.

I must be more exhausted than I realized. Tio Bruno didn't even finish making me go through my drills, so there's that to look forward to tomorrow.

"Cruz," Adelita whimpers, tugging on my heartstrings.

She's on her back, resting her neck over Santos' outstretched arm. Her eyes are closed but her arms reach out for me.

If you insist.

I'm just sleepy enough to be stupid, so I plant small kisses across her forehead and down her cheek as I sink into her arms. My hand ghosts over her stomach, feeling the softness of her abdomen beneath the silk that's teased me since she crawled onto the bed. Her thighs part, but I control myself, biting my lower lip through a moan of pure lust.

I want this woman so badly.

But she's holding onto consciousness by a thread.

The room tilts violently, and another wave of exhaustion nearly takes me under.

"Cruz," she purrs. "Something's wrong."

I'm too tired to rally this time, and finally turn her on her side. Santos is spooning her, and I curl her leg around my waist. I love everything about this, especially when my hand roams to the bare underside of her thigh. I scoot down until I can bury my face in the crook of her neck, where the natural scent of her skin is freshest.

"I'll fix it, baby," I promise with a yawn and a kiss to her throat. "First thing in the morning, I'll fix it all."

I can't fight consciousness another second before I'm taken under.

* * *

MY DREAMS COME on hard in the night. First, there's Adelita, blurred and standing above me with an unfocused look to her usually sharp eyes. She pushes me aside and tugs on... another Adelita. The sleeping beauty in my arms.

I lift my hand to stop one Adelita from taking the other, but I am easy for her to bat aside.

Then both Adelitas exit my bedroom, giving me the sense that something is off.

In what feels like the next breath, the wind changes, bringing a foul and desperate edge to the dream. My spine tingles when I hear the familiar cackle of triumph that always sets my teeth on edge.

"No!" I shout at the old witch. "You can't come for me anymore. I have Addy right with me."

Only she's not there anymore.

La Sayona comes at me with a sickle and a cracked-tooth grin of pure malice. It's not just that she's evil and vindictive, it's that she enjoys my agony.

No matter how fast I run, she always catches me. No matter how brutally I fight, she's always one step ahead of my punches.

I turn and bolt away from her through the fog—always through a fog. My heart pounds like I'm on the verge of a heart attack, but I keep going.

Her sickle catches my shin, ripping my skin to the bone as she trips me. "I've missed you, my boy. My wicked, lonely boy."

"No!" I shout as she rakes the sickle across the back of my thigh, filleting my leg so painfully, I lose my voice to my scream. "Addy! Addy, come back!"

I need her. I need her to save me.

But there's only me, as it's always been, fighting a losing battle in my mind, and wondering where my Addy could have gone.

Love the book? Leave a review.
Otherwise, Adelita dies.

DAMAGED HEARTS

Enjoy a free preview of *Damaged Hearts,*
Book four in the "Savage Hearts" series.

NO PROTECTION

CRUZ

All my favorite things start out as bad ideas.

It was a poor choice to sleep next to Adelita, but I did it anyway. Granted, the first time, I wasn't aware she was so near, but I've invited her into my bed many nights since then, even though I knew it was dangerous.

My mother drove a stake through her own temple to escape the mental torture of La Sayona. The witch who haunted my grandfather also tormented my dad. When I came of age, La Sayona left him and seeped into me. Every night, she chases me, captures me and takes a sickle to my flesh. It's terrifying, so much that I refuse to sleep beside a woman. La Sayona is a jealous witch, zealous in her torment of our bloodline. If she senses I might be near a woman, she will drive my partner to madness.

It's why I never should have let Adelita sleep beside me.

Yet now it's my favorite thing.

Addy's soft skin brushes my face while I sleep, her midnight-colored hair tickling me when she shifts under the covers. She makes precious cooing sounds in her sleep. I know they're precious because I never use that word other than to describe her little sleep sounds.

It's an odd dichotomy of sensations that hit me when I sleep with Addy. Her curvy body looks so trusting in slumber. It makes my chest swell with all the best parts of masculine energy. I want to protect her, to buy her things, to make her smile, to hold her as if she's fragile.

Of course, she's nothing like breakable.

The other feeling I cannot deny is the overwhelming landslide of safety that engulfs me whenever I sleep by her side. I don't know what it is about her that protects me, but that's exactly what she does. La Sayona leaves me if Adelita is by my side.

My Adelita is the strongest person I've ever come across. She can tear the door off a car like it's made of tinfoil.

La Sayona should be scared.

Except tonight, she's not.

I've grown soft, too off my guard. I didn't expect La Sayona to attack tonight, but she's driven stakes into my hands, nailing me to the ground of my psyche so she can peel the skin off my back. I tell myself it's a night terror. I tell myself I'm safe, but the pain is real. Real and inescapable.

It takes a lot to wake me when La Sayona has her hold on my mind, so when water fills my nose and makes me feel like I'm drowning, I am grateful for the relief.

Santos. Santos is here. Santos is waterboarding me, because that's what he does when I can't wake up.

La Sayona screams that her pig is being taken away from her. The witch never tires of punishing the men in my family for the sins of the past.

I cough, choke and splutter as rough hands tip me onto my side. Santos is the nicest guy on the planet, but raised by sadists, so waterboarding me makes logical sense to him.

My entire nasal passage burns, but as my eyes blink the

room into focus, the discomfort is the least of my problems. "What... Huh?" Why Tio Bruno is in my bedroom with Rafi and my father, while Adelita is gone is beyond me.

Santos sits back in the bed, because of course the woman of every man's dream comes with a boyfriend, who just so happens to be my adoptive brother. Santos holds his head in his hands, and when I sit up, I can see why. If his headache is anything like mine, I pity him.

The room spins while I grip the headboard. "Why are you all in my bedroom?" Then, before I can stop myself, I blurt out, "Where's Adelita?"

I'm not supposed to be this attached to her. I've tried to play it off like it was a convenience thing. She chases away La Sayona, so we sleep beside each other. No big deal. Nothing more than a friend helping out a friend.

Except I don't think friends watch each other sleep.

And I really don't think a friend notices when his buddy's nipples are taut and erect.

Shit.

"On your feet!" Tio Bruno's voice comes out like a foghorn. It's like he thinks he's still in the barracks, commanding troops and giving orders laced with unending disappointment.

If I ever found a single thing that might impress my uncle, I would do that thing every day. But as I've actually tried everything in my arsenal and he still looks at me with veiled displeasure, as he's doing right now, I'm not sure he's capable of being pleased.

My dad's cadence tempers the harsh command. "Easy, Bruno. It's clear something happened to them. Quick, Aarón, fetch them some water. The healer's on the way. Are you hurt, boys?"

My closed eyes help me focus, but the second my lids

open, the room spins again. "Ugh. Did we go drinking last night?"

Tio Bruno moves to the nightstand and sniffs our cups. "Milk. What happened? Do you know where they took her?"

"Who?"

Tio Bruno narrows his eyes at me as if he thinks I'm trying to be funny. "Adelita. Did you see who took her?" I look much like him—same shape to my mouth, same hard cut to our jawlines, same broad shoulders, thick chests and towering forms.

Only nothing about me feels towering or strong this morning. My head aches, which, after being tortured all night with a sickle, is just the icing on the cake.

I pinch the bridge of my nose, trying to force Tio Bruno's words to make sense.

Santos tilts his head up at my uncle, and then makes to stand. One step out of the bed, and his legs go out from under him. "Oh!"

Dad dashes to Santos, helping him back into the bed. "Easy, Son." He feels Santos' forehead and frowns. "He's fainted."

I gape at Santos.

Well, I'll be. He did faint.

Rafi rushes to Santos, slapping his cheeks to no avail. "Wake up! Santos, stop this! What happened?"

"Adelita? Where is she?" My mouth is so dry.

Did Adelita get up in the night and get lost on the way back to the bedroom? Is that why La Sayona was able to get to me?

Tio Bruno gets in my face and shouts, "Where is she? Who took her? Focus, Cruz!"

He's wrong. No one could possibly take Adelita. She's strong. She's…

"Cruz!" Tio Bruno barks, shaking my shoulders.

His volume combines with whatever is in my system that's making things blurry. I open my mouth to respond, but the room tilts. Before I know it, my head hits the pillow, and the room goes dark.

Continue the series with *Damaged Hearts* today!

ABOUT THE AUTHOR

USA Today bestselling author Mary E. Twomey lives in Michigan with her three adorable children. She enjoys reading, writing, vegetarian cooking, and telling her children fantastic stories about wombats.

While she loves writing fantasy, dystopian, and paranormal tales for her readers, Mary also writes romance under the name Tuesday Embers.

Visit her online at www.maryetwomey.com, and sign up for her newsletter, so you never miss a new release.